Praise for the novels of Christine Feehan

"Brilliant. The sexual energy . . . is electrifying. If you enjoy paranormal romances, this is a must read."
—*Romance At Heart*

"Having fast made a name for herself in the vampire romance realm, Feehan now turns her attention to other supernatural powers in this swift, sensational offering . . . The sultry, spine-tingling kind of read that [Feehan's] fans will adore." —*Publishers Weekly*

"One of the best current voices in the darker paranormal romance subgenre . . . intense, sensual, and mesmerizing . . . a rising star in paranormal romance."
—*Library Journal*

"Sizzling sex scenes, both physical and telepathic, pave the road to true love . . . Action, suspense, and smart characters make this erotically charged romance an entertaining read." —*Booklist*

Magic in the Wind

CHRISTINE FEEHAN

BERKLEY BOOKS, NEW YORK

THE BERKLEY PUBLISHING GROUP
Published by the Penguin Group
Penguin Group (USA) Inc.
375 Hudson Street, New York, New York 10014, USA
Penguin Group (Canada), 90 Eglinton Avenue East, Suite 700, Toronto, Ontario M4P 2Y3, Canada
(a division of Pearson Penguin Canada Inc.)
Penguin Books Ltd., 80 Strand, London WC2R 0RL, England
Penguin Group Ireland, 25 St. Stephen's Green, Dublin 2, Ireland (a division of Penguin Books Ltd.)
Penguin Group (Australia), 250 Camberwell Road, Camberwell, Victoria 3124, Australia
(a division of Pearson Australia Group Pty. Ltd.)
Penguin Books India Pvt. Ltd., 11 Community Centre, Panchsheel Park, New Delhi—110 017, India
Penguin Group (NZ), Cnr. Airborne and Rosedale Roads, Albany, Auckland 1310, New Zealand
(a division of Pearson New Zealand Ltd.)
Penguin Books (South Africa) (Pty.) Ltd., 24 Sturdee Avenue, Rosebank, Johannesburg 2196,
South Africa

Penguin Books Ltd., Registered Offices: 80 Strand, London WC2R 0RL, England

Previously published in the anthology *Lover Beware*, published by The Berkley Publishing Group.

MAGIC IN THE WIND

A Berkley Book / published by arrangement with the author

PRINTING HISTORY
Berkley edition / October 2005

ISBN: 0-425-20863-X

BERKLEY®
Berkley Books are published by The Berkley Publishing Group,
a division of Penguin Group (USA) Inc.,
375 Hudson Street, New York, New York 10014.
BERKLEY is a registered trademark of Penguin Group (USA) Inc.
The "B" design is a trademark belonging to Penguin Group (USA) Inc.

PRINTED IN THE UNITED STATES OF AMERICA

10 9 8 7 6 5 4 3 2 1

For my sisters . . . Thank you for the magic and the love
that has always been in my life.

Chapter 1

~

"SARAH'S BACK. SARAH'S come home." The whisper was overly loud and tinged with something close to fear. Or respect. Damon Wilder couldn't decide which. He'd been hearing the same small-town gossip for several hours and it was always said in the same hushed tones. He hated to admit to curiosity and he wasn't about to stoop to asking, not after he had made such a point of insisting on absolute privacy since he arrived last month.

As he walked down the quaint narrow sidewalk made of wood, the wind seemed to whisper, "Sarah's back." He heard it as he passed the gas station and burly Jeff Dockins waved to him. He heard it as he lingered in the small bakery. *Sarah.* The name shouldn't carry mystery, but it did.

He had no idea who Sarah was, but she commanded such interest and awe from the townspeople he found himself totally intrigued. He knew from experience the people in the sleepy little coastal town were not easily impressed. No amount of money, fame, or title earned one deference. Everyone was treated the same, from the poorest to the richest, and there seemed to be no prejudice against religion or any other preferences. It was why he had chosen the town. A man could be anybody here and no one cared.

All day he had heard the whispers. He'd never once caught a glimpse of the mysterious Sarah. But he'd heard she'd once climbed the sheer cliffs above the sea to rescue a dog. An impossible task. He'd seen those crumbling cliffs and no one could climb them. He found himself smiling at the idea of anyone attempting such an impossible feat, and few things amused him or intrigued him.

The only grocery store was in the center of town and most of the gossip originated there and then spread like wildfire. Damon decided he needed a few things before he went home. He hadn't been in the store for more than two minutes when he heard it again. "Sarah's back." The same hushed whisper, the same awe and respect.

Inez Nelson, owner of the grocery store, held court, spilling out gossip as she normally did, instead of ringing up the groceries on the cash register. It usually drove him crazy to have to wait, but this time he lingered by the bread rack in the hope of learning more of the mysterious Sarah who had finally returned.

"Are you sure, Inez?" Trudy Garret asked, dragging her four-year-old closer to her and nearly strangling the child with her hug. "Are her sisters back, too?"

"Oh, I'm certain, all right. She came right into the store as real as you please and bought a ton of groceries. She was back at the cliff house, she said. She didn't say anything about the others, but if one shows up the others aren't far behind."

Trudy Garret looked around, lowered her voice another octave. "Was she still . . . Sarah?"

Damon rolled his eyes. Everyone always annoyed the hell out of him. He thought moving to a small town would allow him to find a way to get along to some extent but people were just plain idiots. Of course Sarah was still Sarah. Who the hell else would she be? Sarah was probably the only one with a brain within a fifty-mile radius so they thought she was different.

"What could it mean?" Trudy asked. "Sarah only comes back when something is going to happen."

"I asked her if everything was all right and she just smiled in that way she has and said yes. You wouldn't want me to pry into Sarah's business, now would you, dear," Inez said piously.

Damon let his breath out in a hissing rush of impatience. Inez made it her life's work to pry into everyone's business. Why should the absent Sarah be excluded?

"Last time she was here Dockins nearly died, do you remember that?" Trudy asked. "He fell from his roof and Sarah just happened to be walking by and . . ." She trailed off and glanced around the store and lowered her voice to a conspirator's whisper. "Old Mars at the fruit stand said Penny told him Sarah . . ."

"Trudy, dear, you know Mars is totally unreliable in the things he says. He's a dear, sweet man, but he sometimes makes things up," Inez pointed out.

Old man Mars was crotchety, mean, and known to throw fruit at cars if he was in a foul enough mood. Damon waited for lightning to strike Inez for her blatant lie, but nothing happened. The worst of it was, Damon wanted to know what old Mars had said about Sarah, even if it was a blatant lie. And that really irritated him.

Trudy leaned even closer, looked melodramatically to the right and left without even noticing he was there. Damon sighed heavily, wanting to shake the woman. "Do you remember the time little Paul Baily fell into that blowhole?"

"I remember that, now that you say. He was wedged in so tight and no one could get to him, he'd slipped down so far. The tide was coming in."

"I was there, Inez, I saw her get him out." Trudy straightened up. "Penny said she'd heard from her hairdresser that Sarah was working for a secret agency and she was sent to some foreign country undercover to assassinate the leader of a terrorist group."

"Oh, I don't think so, Trudy. Sarah wouldn't kill anything." The store owner's hands fluttered to her throat in protest. "I just can't imagine."

Damon had had enough of gossip. If they weren't going to say anything worth hearing, he was going to get the hell out of there before Inez turned her spotlight on him. He plunked his groceries down on the counter and looked as bored as he could manage. "I'm in a hurry, Inez," he said, hoping to facilitate matters and avoid Inez's usual attempts at matchmaking.

"Why, Damon Wilder, how lovely to see you. Have you met Trudy Garret? Trudy is a wonderful woman, a native of our town. She works over at the Salt Bar and Grill. Have you been there to eat yet? The salmon is very good."

"So I've heard," he muttered, barely glancing at Trudy to acknowledge the introduction. It didn't matter. They'd all made up their minds about him, making up the history he refused to provide. He felt a little sorry for the returning Sarah. They were making up things about her as well. "You might tell me about that beautiful old house on the cliffs," he said, shocking himself. Shocking Inez. He never gave anyone an opening for conversation. He wanted to be left alone. Damn Sarah for being so mysterious.

Inez looked as if she might faint and for once she was speechless.

"You must know the one I'm talking about," Damon persisted, in spite of himself. "Three stories, balconies everywhere, a round turret. It's grown over quite wild around the house, but there's a path leading to the old lighthouse. I was walking up there and with all the wild growth, I expected the house to be in bad shape, dilapidated like most of the abandoned homes around here, but it was in beautiful condition. I'd like to know what preservatives were used."

"That's private property, Mr. Wilder," Inez said. "The house has been in the same family for well over a hundred years. I don't know what they use in the paint, but it does weather well. No one lurks around that house." Inez was definitely issuing a reprimand to him.

"I was hardly lurking, Inez," he said, exasperated. "As you well know, the sea salt is hard on the paint and wood of the houses. That house is in remarkable condition. In fact, it looks newly built. I'm curious as to what was used. I'd like to preserve my house in the same way." He made an effort to sound reasonable instead of annoyed. "I'm a bit of a chemist and I can't figure out what would keep a house so pristine over the years. There's no sign of damage from the sea, from age, or even insects. Remarkable."

Inez pursed her lips, always a bad sign. "Well, I'm certain I have no idea." Her voice was stiff, as if she were highly offended. She rang up his groceries in remarkable time without saying another word.

Damon gathered the bags into one arm, his expression daring Inez to ask him if he needed help. Leaning heavily on his cane, he turned to Trudy. "The hairdresser's dog walker told the street cleaner that he saw Sarah walk on water."

Trudy's eyes widened in shock, but there was belief on her face. Inez made some kind of noise he couldn't identify. Disgusted, Damon turned on his heel and stalked out. Ever since the first whisper of Sarah's name he had been unsettled. Disturbed. Agitated. There was something unfamiliar growing inside of him. Anticipation? Excitement? That was ridiculous. He muttered a curse under his breath at the absent Sarah.

He wanted to be left alone, didn't he? He had no interest in the woman the townspeople gossiped about. Sarah might not walk on water but her house was a mystery. He saw no reason why he shouldn't pay her a neighborly visit and ask what preservatives were used in the wood to achieve the nearly impossible results.

Damon Wilder was a man driven to the edge of sanity. Moving to this tiny town on the coast was his last effort to hang onto life. He had no idea how he was going to do it, or why he had chosen this particular town with all its resident eccentrics, but he had been drawn here. Nothing else would do. He had stepped on the rich soil and knew either this place would be home or he had none. It was hell trying to fit in, but the sea soothed him and the long walks over million-year-old rocks and cliffs occupied his mind.

Damon took his time putting his groceries away. The knowledge that this town, this place, was his last stand had been so strong he had actually purchased a house. His home was one of the few things that gave him pleasure. He loved working on it. He loved the wood. He could lose himself in the artistry of reshaping a room to suit his exact needs. For hours at a time the work occupied him such that nothing else could invade his brain and he was at peace for a time.

He stared out his large bay window, the one that looked out over the sea. The one that had an unobstructed view of the house on the cliff. Damon had spent more hours than he cared to think about staring up at the dark silent windows and the balconies and battlements. It was a unique house from another century, another time and place. There were lights on for the first time. The windows shone a bright welcome.

His leg hurt like hell. He needed to sit and rest, not go traipsing around the countryside. Damon stared at the house, drawn to the warmth of it. It seemed almost alive, begging him to come closer. He went outside onto his deck, intending to sit in the chair and enjoy his view of the sea. Instead he found himself limping his way steadily up the path toward the cliffs. It was nearly a compulsion. The path was narrow and steep and rocky in places, almost no more than a deer trail and overgrown at that. His cane slipped on the pebbles and twice he nearly fell. He was swearing by the time he made it to the edge of the private property.

He stood there staring in shock. Damon had been there not two days before, walking around the house and the grounds. It had been wildly overgrown, the bushes high and weeds everywhere. The shrubbery and trees had drooped with winter darkness on the leaves. A noticeable absence of sound had given the place an eerie, creepy feeling. Now there were flowers, as if everything had burst into blossom overnight. A riot of color met his eyes, a carpet of grass was beneath his feet. He could hear the insects buzzing, the sound of frogs calling merrily back and forth as if spring had come instantly.

The gate, which had been securely locked, stood open in welcome. Everything seemed to be welcoming him. A sense of peace began to steal into his heart. A part of him wanted to sit on one of the inviting benches and soak in the atmosphere.

Roses climbed the trellis and rhododendrons were everywhere, great forests of them. He'd never seen such towering plants. Damon started up the pathway, noting every single weed was gone. Stepping stones led the way to the house. Each round of stone held a meticulously carved symbol. Great care had been taken to etch the symbol deep into the stone. Damon leaned down to feel the highly polished work. He admired the craftsmanship and detail. The artisans in the small town all had that trait, one he greatly respected.

As he neared the house, a wind rose off the sea and carried sea spray and a lilting melody. *"Sarah's back. Sarah's home."* The words sang across the land joyously. It was then he heard the birds and looked around him. They were everywhere, all kinds of birds, flitting from tree to tree, a flutter of wings overhead. Squirrels chattered as they rushed from branch to branch. The sun was sinking over the ocean, turning the sky into bright colors of pink and orange and red. The fog was on the far horizon, meeting the sea to give the impression of an island in the clouds. Damon had never seen anything so beautiful. He simply stood there, leaning on his cane and staring in wonder at the transformation around him.

Voices drifted from the house. One was soft and melodious. He couldn't catch the words but the tone worked its way through his skin into his very bones. Into his vital organs. He moved closer, drawn by the sound, and immediately saw two dogs on the front porch. Both were watching him alertly, heads down, hair up, neither making a sound.

Damon froze. The voices continued. One was weeping. He could hear the heartbreaking sound. A woman's voice. The melodious voice soothed. Damon shifted his weight and took a two-handed grip on his cane. If he had to use it as a weapon, that would give him more leverage. Concerned though he was with the dogs, he was more centered on the voice. He strained to listen.

"Please, Sarah, you have to be able to do something. I know you can. Please say you'll help me. I can't bear this," the crying voice said.

Her sorrow was so deep Damon ached for her. He couldn't remember the last time he'd felt someone's pain. He couldn't remember how to feel anything but bored or frustrated. The dogs both sniffed the air and, as if recognizing him, wagged their tails in greeting and sat down, hair settling to make them appear much more friendly. Keeping one eye on the dogs, he strained to catch the words spoken in that soft lilting tone.

"I know it's difficult, Irene, but this isn't something like putting a Band-Aid on a scraped knee. What do the doctors say?"

There was more sobbing. It shook him, hurt him, tore up his insides so that his gut churned and a terrible weight pressed on his chest. Damon forgot all about the dogs and pressed his hand over his heart. Irene Madison. Now he recognized the voice, knew from Inez at the grocery store that her fifteen-year-old son, Drew, was terminally ill.

"There's no hope, Sarah. They said to take him home and

make him comfortable. You know you can find a way. Please do this for us, for me."

Damon edged closer to the house, wondering what the hell she thought Sarah could do. Work a miracle? There was a small silence. The window was open, the wind setting the white lacy curtains dancing. He waited, holding his breath. Waited for Sarah's answer. Waited for the sound of her voice.

"Irene, you know I don't do that sort of thing. I've only just come back. I haven't even unpacked. You're asking me . . ."

"Sarah, I'm begging you. I'll do anything, give you anything. I'm begging on my knees . . ." The sobs were choking Damon. The pain was so raw in the woman.

"Irene, get up! What are you doing? Stop it."

"You have to say you'll come to see him. Please, Sarah. Our mothers were best friends. If not for me, do it for my mother."

"I'll come by, Irene. I'm not promising anything, but I'll stop by." There was resignation in that gentle voice. Weariness. "My sisters will be coming in a day or so and as soon as we're all rested we'll stop by and see what we can do."

"I know you think I'm asking for a miracle, but I'm not, I just want more time with him. Come when you're rested, when the others have come and can help." The relief Irene felt spilled over to Damon and he had no clue why. Only that the weight pressing on his chest lifted and his heart soared for a moment.

"I'll see what I can do."

The voices were traveling toward him. Damon waited, his heart pounding in anticipation. He had no idea what to expect or even what he wanted, but everything in him stilled.

The door opened and two women emerged to stand in the shadow of the wide, columned porch. "Thank you, Sarah. Thank you so much," Irene said, clutching at Sarah's hands gratefully. "I knew you would come." She hurried down the stairs, straight past the dogs, who had rushed to their mistress. Irene managed a quick smile for Damon as she passed him, her tearstained face bright with hope.

Damon leaned on his cane and stared up at Sarah.

Chapter 2

⌒

SARAH STOOD ON the porch, her body in the shadows. Damon had no idea of her age. Her face seemed timeless. Her eyes were old eyes, filled with intelligence and power. Her skin was smooth and flawless, giving her the appearance of extreme youth, very much at odds with the knowledge in her direct gaze. She simply stood there quietly, her incredible eyes fixed on him.

"How did you get through the gate?"

It wasn't what he expected. Damon half turned to look back at the wrought-iron masterpiece of art. The gate was six feet high and an intricate piece of craftsmanship. He had studied it on more than one occasion, noting the symbols and depictions of various animals and stars and moons. A collage of creatures with raw power mixed with universal signs of the earth, water, fire, and wind. Always before when he had come to stare at the house and grounds the gate had been firmly locked.

"It was open," he replied simply.

Her eyebrow shot up and she looked from him to the gate and back again. There was interest in her gaze. "And the dogs?" Her hand dropped to one massive head as she absently scratched the ears.

"They gave me the once-over and decided I was friendly," he answered.

A faint frown touched her face, was gone in an instant. "Did they? You must get along well with animals."

"I don't get along well with anything," he blurted out before he could stop himself. He was so shocked and embarrassed at the admission he couldn't find a way to laugh it off, so it remained there between them.

Sarah simply studied his face for a long while. An eternity. She had a direct gaze that seemed to see past his physical body and delve straight to his soul. It made Damon uncomfortable and ashamed. "You'd better come in and sit down for a while," she said. "There's a blackness around your aura. I can tell you're in pain, although I can't see why you've come yet." She turned and went into the house, clearly expecting him to follow her. Both dogs did, hurrying after her, pacing at her heels.

Damon had been acting out of character ever since he heard that first whisper of gossip. He stood, leaning on his cane, wondering what had gotten into him. He'd seen the mighty Sarah. She was just a woman with incredible eyes. That was all. She couldn't walk on water or move mountains. She couldn't scale impossible cliffs or assassinate heads of terrorist organizations. She was just a woman. And probably as loony as hell. His aura was black? What the hell did that mean? She probably had voodoo dolls and dead chickens in her house.

He stared at the open door. She didn't come back or look to see if he was following. The house had swallowed her up. Mysterious Sarah. Damon lifted his eyes to the gathering darkness, to the first stars and the floating wisps of clouds. It irritated him but he knew he was going to follow her into that house. Just like her damn dogs.

Damon consoled himself with the fact that he was extremely interested in the preservation of wood and paint. He had been interested in her house long before she arrived back in town. He couldn't pass up a genuine opportunity to study it up close, even if it meant trying to make small talk with a crazy stranger. He raked his hand through his dark hair and glared at the empty doorway. Muttering curses beneath his breath, he stalked after her as best he could with his cane and his damaged hip and leg.

The porch stairs were as solid as a rock. The verandah itself was wide and beautiful, wrapping around the house, an invitation to sit in the shade and enjoy the view of the pounding sea. Damon wanted to linger there and continue to feel the peace of Sarah's home, but he stepped inside. The air seemed cool and scented, smelling of some fragrance that reminded him of the forests and flowers. The entryway was wide, tiled with a mosaic design, and it opened into a huge room.

With a sense of awe, Damon stared down at the artwork on the floor. There was a feeling of falling into another world when he looked at it. The deep blue of the sea was really the ocean in the sky. Stars burst and flared into life. The moon was a shining ball of silver. He stood transfixed, wanting to get on his knees and examine every inch of the floor. "I like this floor. It's a shame to walk on it," he announced loudly.

"I'm glad you like it. I think it's beautiful," she said. Her voice was velvet soft, but it carried through the house back to him. "My grandmother and her sisters made that together. It took them a very long time to get it just right. Tell me what you see when you look into the midnight sky there."

He hesitated but the pull of the floor was too much to resist. He examined it carefully. "There are dark shadows in the clouds across the moon. And behind the clouds, a ring of red surrounds the moon. The stars connect and make a bizarre pattern. The body of a man is floating on the sea of clouds and something has pierced his heart." He looked up at her, a challenge on his face.

Sarah merely smiled. "I was about to have tea; would you care for a cup?" She walked away from him into the open kitchen.

Damon could hear the sound of water as she filled the teakettle. "Yes, thank you, that sounds good." And it did, which was crazy. He never drank tea. Not a single cup. He was losing his mind.

"The pictures of my grandmother and her sisters are to your left, if you'd like to see them."

He had always considered looking at pictures of people he didn't know utterly ridiculous, but he couldn't resist looking at the photographs of the women who had managed to create such beauty on a floor. He wandered over to the wall of memories. There were many photographs of women, some black-

and-white, others in color. Some of the pictures were obviously very old, but he could easily see the resemblance among the women. Damon cleared his throat. He frowned when he noticed a strange pattern running through every grouping. "Why are there seven women in each family picture?"

"There seems to be a strange phenomenon in our family," Sarah answered readily. "Every generation, someone produces seven daughters."

Startled, Damon leaned on his cane and studied each group of faces. "One out of the seven girls has always given birth to seven daughters? On purpose?"

Sarah laughed and came around the corner to join him in front of the wall of photographs. "Every generation."

He looked from her to the faces of her sisters in a picture near the center of the wall. "Which one carries the strain of insanity?"

"Good question. No one's ever thought to ask it before. My sister Elle is the seventh daughter so she inherits the mantle of responsibility. Or insanity, if you prefer." Sarah pointed to a girl with a young face, vivid green eyes, and a wealth of red hair pulled carelessly into a ponytail.

"And where is poor Elle right now?" Damon asked.

Sarah inhaled, then let her breath out slowly, her long lashes fluttering down. At once her face was in repose. She looked tranquil, radiant. Watching her did something funny to Damon's heart, a curious melting sensation that was utterly terrifying. He couldn't take his fascinated gaze off of her. Strangely, for just one moment, he felt as if Sarah was no longer in the room with him. As if her physical body had separated from her spirit, allowing her to travel across time and space. Damon shook himself, trying to get rid of the crazy impression. He wasn't an imaginative person, yet he was certain Sarah had somehow touched her sister Elle.

"Elle is in a cave of gems, deep under the ground where she can hear the heartbeat of the earth." Sarah opened her eyes and looked at him. "I'm Sarah Drake."

"Damon Wilder." He gestured toward his house. "Your new neighbor." He was staring at her, drinking her in. It didn't make sense. He was certain she wasn't the most beautiful woman in the world but his heart and lungs were insisting she was. Sarah was average height, with a woman's figure. She wore faded, worn blue jeans and a plaid flannel shirt. She certainly was not at all glamorous, yet his lungs burned for air and his heart accelerated. His body hardened painfully when she wasn't even trying to be a sexy siren, simply standing there in her comfortable old clothes with her wealth of dark hair pulled back from her pale face. It was the most infuriating and humiliating thing it was his misfortune to endure.

"You bought the old Hanover place. The view is fantastic. How did you come to find our little town?" Her cool blue gaze was direct and far too assessing. "You look like a man who would be far more comfortable in a big city."

Damon's fist tightened around his cane. Sarah could see his knuckles were white. "I saw it on a map and just knew it was the place I wanted to live in when I retired." She studied his face, the lines of suffering etched into his face, the too old eyes. He was surrounded with the mark of Death, and he read Death in the midnight sky, yet she was strangely drawn to him.

Her eyebrow went up, a perfect arch. "You're a little young to retire, I would have thought. There's not a lot of excitement here."

"I'll have to disagree with that. Have you hung out around the grocery store lately? Inez provides amazing entertainment." There was a wealth of sarcasm mixed with contempt in his voice.

Sarah turned away from him, her shoulders stiffening visibly. "What do you actually know about Inez to have managed to form an opinion in your month of living here?" She sounded sweet and interested but he had the feeling he had just stepped hard on her toes.

Damon limped after her like a puppy dog, trying not to mutter foul curses under his breath. It never mattered to him what other people thought. Everyone had opinions and few actually had educated ones. Why the hell did Sarah's opinion of him matter? And why did her hips have to sway with mesmerizing invitation?

The kitchen was tiled with the same midnight blue that had formed the sky in the mosaic. A long bank of windows looked out over a garden of flowers and herbs. He could see a three-tiered fountain in the middle of the courtyard. Sarah waved him toward the long table while she fixed the tea. Damon couldn't see a speck of dust or dirt anywhere in the house. "When did you arrive?"

"Late last night. It feels wonderful to be home again. It's been a couple of years since my last visit. My parents are in Europe at the moment. They own several homes and love Italy. My grandmother is with them, so the cliff house has been empty."

"So this is your parents' home?" When she shook her head with her slight, mysterious smile he asked, "Do you own this house?"

"With my sisters. It was given to us through our mother." She brought a steaming mug of tea and placed it on the table beside his hand. "I think you'll like this. It's soothing and will help take away the pain."

"I didn't say I was in pain." Damon could have kicked himself. Even to his own ears he sounded ridiculous, a defiant child denying the truth. "Thank you," he managed to mutter, trying to smell the tea without offending her.

Sarah sat across from him, cradling a teacup between her palms. "How can I help you, Mr. Wilder?"

"Call me Damon," he said.

"Damon then," she acknowledged with a small smile. "I'm just Sarah."

Damon could feel her penetrating gaze. "I've been very interested in your house, Sarah. The paint hasn't faded or peeled, not even in the salt air. I was hoping you would tell me what preservative you used."

Sarah leaned back in her chair, brought the teacup to her mouth. She had a beautiful mouth. Wide and full and curved as if she laughed all the time. Or invited kisses. The thought came unbidden as he stared at her mouth. Sheer temptation. Damon felt the weight of her gaze. Color began to creep up the back of his neck.

"I see. You came out late in the evening even though you were hurting because you were anxious to know what kind of preservative I use on my house. That certainly makes perfect sense."

There was no amusement in her voice, not even a hint of sarcasm, but the dull red color spread to his face. Her eyes saw too much, saw into him where he didn't want to be seen, where he couldn't afford to be seen. He wanted to look away but he couldn't seem to pull his gaze from hers.

"Tell me why you're really here." Her voice was soft, inviting confidence.

He raked both hands through his hair in frustration. "I honestly don't know. I'm sorry for invading your privacy." But he wasn't. It was a lie and they both knew it.

She took another sip of tea and gestured toward his mug. "Drink it. It's a special blend I make myself. I think you'll like it and I know it will make you feel better." She grinned at him. "I can promise you there aren't any toads or eye of newt in it."

Sarah's smile robbed him of breath immediately. It was a strange thing to feel a punch in the gut so hard it drove the air out of one's lungs just with a simple smile. He waited several heartbeats until he recovered enough to speak. "Why do you think I need to feel better?" he asked, striving for nonchalance.

"I don't have to be a seer for that, Damon. You're limping. There are white lines around your mouth and your leg is trembling."

Damon raised the cup to his mouth, took a cautious sip of the brew. The taste was unique. "I was attacked awhile back." The words emerged before he could stop them. Horrified, he stared into the tea mug, afraid her brew was a truth serum.

Sarah put her teacup carefully on the table. "A person attacked you?"

"Well, he wasn't an alien." He swallowed a gulp of tea. The heat warmed him, spreading through his body to reach sore, painful places.

"Why would one man want to kill another?" Sarah mused aloud. "I've never understood that. Money is such a silly reason really."

"Most people don't think so." He rubbed his head as if it hurt, or maybe in memory. "People kill for all sorts of reasons, Sarah."

"How awful for you. I hope he was caught."

Before he could stop himself, Damon shook his head. Her vivid gaze settled on his face, looked inside of him again until he wanted to curse. "I was able to get away, but my assistant"—he stopped, corrected himself—"my friend wasn't so lucky."

"Oh, Damon, I'm so sorry."

"I don't want to think about it." He couldn't. It was too close, too raw. Still in his nightmares, still in his heart and soul. He could hear the echoes of screams. He could see the pleading in Dan Treadway's eyes. He would carry that sight to his death, forever etched in his brain. At once the pain was almost too much to bear. He wept inside, his chest burning, his throat clogging with grief.

Sarah reached across the table to place her fingertips on his head. The gesture seemed natural, casual even, and her touch was so light he barely felt it. Yet he felt the results like shooting stars bursting through his brain. Tiny electrical impulses that blasted away the terrible throbbing in his temples and the back of his neck.

He caught her wrists, pulled her hands away from him. He was shaking and she could feel it. "Don't. Don't do that." He released her immediately.

"I'm sorry, I should have asked first," Sarah said. "I was only trying to help you. Would you like me to take you home? It's already dark outside and it wouldn't be safe for you to try to go down the hill without adequate light."

"So I take it the paint preservative is a deep dark family secret," Damon said, attempting to lighten the situation. He drained the tea mug and stood up. "Yes, thanks, I wouldn't mind a ride." It was hard on the ego to have to accept it but he wasn't a complete fool. Could he have behaved any more like an idiot?

Sarah's soft laughter startled him. "I actually don't know whether the preservative is a family secret or not. I'll have to do a little research on the subject and get back to you."

Damon couldn't help smiling just because she was. There was something contagious about Sarah's laughter, something addictive about her personality. "Did you know that when you came home, the wind actually whispered, 'Sarah's back. Sarah's home.' I heard it myself." The words slipped out, almost a tribute.

She didn't laugh at him as he expected. She looked pleased. "What a beautiful thing to say. Thank you, Damon," she said sincerely. "Was the gate really open? The front gate with all the artwork? Not the side gate?"

"Yes, it was standing wide open welcoming me. At least that's how it felt."

Her sea blue eyes drifted over his face, taking in every detail, every line. He knew he wasn't much to look at. A man in his forties, battered and scarred by life. The scars didn't show physically but they went deep and she could clearly see the tormented man. "How very interesting. I think we're destined to be friends, Damon." Her voice wrapped him up in silk and heat.

Damon could see why the townspeople said her name with awe. With respect. Mysterious Sarah. She seemed so open, yet her eyes held a thousand secrets. There was music in her voice and healing in her hands. "I'm glad you've come home, Sarah," he said, hoping he wasn't making more of a fool of himself.

"So am I," she answered.

Chapter 3

"SARAH!" HANNAH DRAKE threw herself into her sister's arms. "It's so good to see you. I missed you so much." She drew back, stretching her arms to full length, the better to examine Sarah. "Why, Sarah, you look like a cat burglar, ready to rob the local museum. I had no idea Frank Warner's paintings had become valuable." She laughed merrily at her own joke.

Sarah's soft laughter merged with Hannah's. "I should have known you'd come creeping in at two A.M. That's so you, Hannah. Where were you this time?"

"Egypt. What an absolutely beautiful country it is." Hannah sat on the porch swing wearily. "But I'm wiped out. I've been traveling forever to get back home." She regarded Sarah's sleek black outfit with a slight frown. "Interesting set of tools you're sporting there, sister mine. I'm not going to have to bail you out of jail, am I? I'm really tired and if the police have to call, I might not wake up."

Sarah adjusted the belt of small tools slung low on her waist without a hint of embarrassment. "If I can't charm a police officer out of booking me for a little break-in, I don't deserve the name Drake. Go on in, Hannah, and go to bed. I'm worried about our neighbor and think I'll just go scout around and make certain nothing happens to him."

Hannah's eyebrow shot up. "Good heavens, Sarah. A man? There's an honest-to-God man in your life? Where is he? I want to go with you." She clasped her hands together, her face radiant. "Wait until I tell the others. The mighty Sarah has fallen!"

"I have *not* fallen—don't start, Hannah. I just have one of my hunches and I'm going to check it out. It has nothing to do with Damon at all."

"Ooh, this is really getting interesting. Damon. You remember his name. How did you meet him? Spill it, Sarah, every last detail!"

"There's nothing to spill. He just waltzed in asking about paint and wood preservatives." Sarah's tone was cool and aloof.

"You want me to believe he walked in on his own without an invitation? You had to have asked him to the house."

"No, I didn't," Sarah denied. "As a matter of fact the gate was open and the dogs allowed him in."

"The gate was open on its own?" Hannah was incredulous. She jumped to her feet. "I'm going with you for certain!"

"No, you're not, you're exhausted, remember?"

"Wait until I tell the others the gate opened for him." Hannah raised her arms to the heavens and stars. "The gate opens for the right man, doesn't it? Isn't that how it works? The gate will swing open in welcome for the man who is destined to become the love of the eldest child's life."

"I don't believe in that nonsense and you know it." Sarah tried to glare but found herself laughing. "I can't believe you'd even think of that old prophecy."

"Like you didn't think of it yourself," Hannah teased. "You're just going off to do the neighborly thing in the middle of the night and just sort of scout around his house. If you say so, of course I'll believe it. Is that telescope up on the battlement directed toward his bedroom?"

"Don't you dare look," Sarah ordered.

Hannah studied her face. "You're laughing but your eyes aren't. What's wrong, Sarah?" She put her hand on her sister's shoulder. "Tell me."

Sarah frowned. "He carries Death on him. I've seen it. And

he read it in the mosaic. I don't know whose death, but I'm drawn to him. His heart is broken and pierced through, and the weight of carrying Death is slowly crushing him. He saw a red ring around the moon."

"Violence and death surround him," Hannah said softly, almost to herself. "Why are you going alone?"

"I have to. I feel . . ." Sarah searched for the right word. "Drawn. It's more than a job, Hannah. It's him."

"He could be dangerous."

"He's surrounded by danger, but if he's dangerous to me, it isn't in the way you're thinking."

"Oh my gosh, you really do like this guy. You think he's hot. I'm telling the others and I'm going up to the battlement to check him out!" Hannah turned and raced into the house, banging the screen door so Sarah couldn't follow her.

Sarah laughed as she blew a kiss to her sister and started down the stairs. Hannah looked wonderful as always. Tall and tanned and beautiful even after traveling across the sea. If her wavy hair was tousled, she just looked in vogue. Other women paid fortunes to try to achieve her natural wind-blown style. Sarah had always been uncommonly proud of Hannah's genuine elegance. She had a bright spirit that shone like the stars overhead. Hannah had a free spirit that longed for wide-open spaces and the wonders of the world. She spoke several languages and traveled extensively. One month she might be found in the pages of a magazine with the jet-setters, the next she was on a dig in Cairo. Her tall slender carriage and incredibly beautiful face made her sought after by every magazine and fashion designer. It was her gentle personality that always drew people to her. Sarah was happy she was home.

Sarah made little sound as she made her way down the small deer path that cut through her property to Damon Wilder's. She knew every inch of her property. And she knew every inch of his. Her hair was tightly braided to keep it from being snagged on low branches or brambles. Her soft-soled shoes were light, allowing her to feel her way over twigs and dried leaves. She wasn't thinking about Damon's broad shoulders or his dark, tormented eyes. And she didn't believe in romance. Not for Sarah. That was for elegant Hannah or beautiful Joley. Well, maybe not the beautiful, *wild* Joley, but definitely for most of her other sisters. Just not Sarah.

Damon Wilder was in trouble in more ways than he knew. Sarah didn't like complications. Ancient prophecies and broad shoulders and black auras were definite complications. Moonlight spilled over the sea as she made her way along the cliffs, following the narrow deer path that eventually wound down the back side of Damon's property. The powerful waves boomed as they rushed and ebbed and collapsed in a froth of white. Sarah found the sound of the sea soothing, even when it raged in a storm. She belonged there, had always belonged, as had her family before her. She didn't fear the sea or the wilds of the countryside, yet her heart was pounding in sudden alarm. Pounding with absolute knowledge.

She was not alone in the night. Instinctively she lowered her body so she wouldn't be silhouetted against the horizon. She used more care, blending into the shadows, using the foliage for cover. She moved with stealth. She was used to secrecy, a highly trained professional. There was no sound as the branches slid away from her tightly knit jumpsuit and her crepe-soled shoes eased over the ground.

Sarah made her way to the outskirts of the house. She knew all about Damon Wilder. One of the smartest men on the planet. A government's treasure. The one-man think tank that had come up with one of the most innovative defense systems ever conceived. His ideas were pure genius, far ahead of their time. He was a steady, focused man. A perfectionist who never overlooked the smallest detail.

When she read about him, before accepting her watchdog assignment, Sarah had been impressed with the sheer tenacity of his character. Now that she had met him, she ached for the man, for the horror of what he had been through. She never allowed her work to be personal, yet she couldn't stop thinking about his eyes and the torment she could see in their dark depths. And she couldn't help but wonder why Death had attached itself to him and was clinging with greedy claws.

Sarah rarely accepted such an assignment, but she knew her cover couldn't have been more perfect. Meant to be. That gave her a slight flutter of apprehension. Destiny, fate, whatever one wanted to call it, was a force to be reckoned with in her family and she had managed to avoid it carefully for years. Damon Wilder had chosen her hometown to settle in. What did that mean? Sarah didn't believe in such close coincidence.

She had no time to circle the house or check the coastal road. As she approached the side of the house facing her home, she heard a muffled curse coming from her left. Sarah inched that way, dropped to her belly, lying flat out in the darker shadows of the trees. She lifted her head cautiously, only her eyes moving restlessly, continually, examining the landscape. It took a few moments to locate her adversaries. She could make out two men not more than forty feet from her, on the downhill, right in the middle of the densest brush. Sarah had the urge to smile. She hoped for their sakes they were wearing their dogs' tick collars.

Lying in the shrubs, she began a slow, complicated pattern with her hands, a flowing dance of fingers while the leaves rustled and twigs began to move as if coming alive. Tiny, silent creatures dropped from branches overhead, fell from leaves, and pushed up from the ground to migrate downhill toward the thickest brush.

Sarah knew that the one window lit up in Damon's house was a bedroom. If the telescope set up on the battlements of her house happened to be pointed in that direction, it was only because it was the last room she had investigated. It just so happened that it was Damon's bedroom, a complete coincidence. Sarah glanced back at her house overlooking the pounding waves, suddenly worried that Hannah might have her eye glued to the lens.

She hissed softly, melodiously, an almost silent note of command the wind caught and carried skyward toward the sea, toward the house on the cliff. The brush of material against wood and leaves attracted her immediate attention. She watched one of the men scuttle like a crab down the hill toward Damon's house. He crouched just below the lit window, then cautiously raised his head to look inside.

The window was raised a few inches to allow the ocean air inside. The breeze blew the kettle cloth drapes inward so that they performed a strange ghoulish dance. With the fluttering curtains it was nearly impossible to get a clear glimpse of the interior. The man half stood, flattening his body against the wall, tilting his head to peer inside.

Sarah could make out the second man lying prone, his rifle directed at the window. She inched her way across the low grasses, moving with the wind as it blew over the land. The

man with his rifle trained on the window never took his gaze
from his target. Never flinched, the gun rock steady. A pro,
then; she had expected it but had hoped otherwise. She could
see the tiny insects crawling into his clothing.

Above her head the clouds were drifting away from the
moon, threatening to expose her completely. She wormed her
way through the grass and brambles, gaining a few more feet.
Sarah pulled her gun from her shoulder holster.

Hearing a slight noise from inside the room, the assailant
at the window put up his hand in warning. He peered in the
window in an attempt to locate Damon. A solid thunk sounded
loud as Damon's cane landed solidly on his jaw. At once the
man screamed, the high-pitched cry reverberating through the
night. He fell backward onto the ground, holding his face,
rolling and writhing in pain.

Sarah kept her gaze fixed on the partner with the rifle. He
was waiting for Damon to expose himself at the window. Damon was too smart to do such an idiotic thing. The curtains
continued their macabre dancing but nothing else stirred in the
night. The moans continued from beneath the window but the
assailant didn't get to his feet.

The rifleman crawled forward on his belly, slipping in the
wet grass so that he rolled, protecting his rifle. It was the slip
Sarah was waiting for. She was on him immediately, pressing
her gun into the back of his neck.

"I suggest you remain very still," she said softly. "You're
trespassing on private property and we just don't like that sort
of thing around here." As she spoke, she kept a wary eye on
the man by the window. She raised her voice. "Damon, have
you called the sheriff? You've got a couple of night visitors
out here that may need a place to stay for a few days and I
heard the jail was empty tonight."

"Is that you, Sarah?"

"I was taking a little stroll and saw a high-powered rifle
kind of lying around in the dirt." She kicked the rifle out of
the captured man's hands. "It's truly a thing of beauty; I just
couldn't pass up the opportunity to get a good look at it."
There was a hint of laughter in her voice, but the muzzle of
her gun remained very firmly pressed against her captive's
neck. "You should stay right there, Damon. There's two of
them out here and they look a bit aggravated." She leaned

close to the man on the ground, but kept her eyes on his partner by the window. "You might want to check yourself the
minute you're in jail. You're probably crawling with ticks.
Nasty little bugs, they burrow in, drink your blood, and pass
on all sorts of interesting things, from staph to Lyme disease.
That bush you were hiding in is lousy with them."

Her heart was still pounding out a rhythm of warning. Then
she knew. Sarah flung herself to her right, rolling away, even
as she heard the whine of bullets zinging past her and thudding
into the ground. Of course there had to be a third man, a driver
waiting in the darkness up on the road. She had been unable
to scout out the land properly. It made perfect sense they
would have a driver, a backup should there be need.

The man next to her scrambled up and dove on top of her,
making a grab for her gun. Sarah managed to get one bent leg
into his stomach to launch him over her head. She felt the
sting of her earlobe as her earring, tangled in his shirt, was
jerked from her ear. He swore viciously as he picked himself
up and raced away from her toward the road. The one closest
to the house was already in motion, staggering up the hill, still
holding his jaw in his hands. The driver provided cover, pin-
ning her down with a spray of bullets. The silencer indicated
the men had no desire to announce their presence to the townspeople.

"Sarah? You all right out there?" Damon called anxiously.
Even with the silencer, he couldn't fail to hear the telltale
whine of bullets.

"Yes." She was disgusted with herself. She could hear the
motor of the car roar to life, the wheels spinning in dirt for a
moment before they caught and the vehicle raced away down
the coastal highway. "I'm sorry, Damon, I let them get away."

"*You're* sorry! You could have been killed, Sarah. And no,
I didn't call the sheriff. I was hoping they were neighborhood
kids looking to do a prank."

"And I took you for such a brilliant man, too," she teased,
sitting up and pulling twigs out of her hair. She touched her
stinging ear, came away with blood on her fingers. It was her
favorite earring, too.

The drapes rustled and Damon poked his head out the window. "Are we going to call back and forth or are you going

to come in here and talk with me." There was more demand than question in his voice.

Sarah laughed softly. "Do you think that's such a good idea? Can you imagine what Inez would say if she knew I was visiting you in the middle of the night?" She reached for the rifle, taking care to pick it up using a handkerchief. "She'd ask you your intentions. You'd have to deny you had any. The word would spread that you'd ruined me and I'd be pitied. I couldn't take that. It's better if I just slink home quietly."

Damon leaned farther out the window. "Damn it, Sarah, I'm not amused. You could have been killed. Do you even understand that? These men were dangerous and you're out taking a little stroll in the moonlight and playing neighborhood cop." His voice was harsher than he intended, but she'd scared the hell out of him. He rubbed a hand over his face, feeling sick at the thought of her in danger.

"I wasn't in any danger, Damon," Sarah assured him. "This rifle, in case you're interested, has tranqs in it, not bullets. At least they weren't trying to kill you, they wanted you alive."

He sighed. She was just sitting there on the ground with the sliver of moonlight spilling over her. The rifle was lying across her knees and she was smiling at him. Sarah's smile was enough to stop a man's heart. Damon took a good look at her clothes, at the gun still in her hand. He stiffened, swore softly. "Damn you anyway, Drake. I should have known you were too good to be true!"

"Were you believing all the stories about me, after all, Damon?" she asked. But dread was beginning even though it shouldn't matter what he thought of her. Or what he knew. She had a job. It shouldn't matter, yet she felt the weight in her chest, heavy like a stone. She felt a sudden fear crawling in her stomach of losing something special before it even started.

"Who sent you, Sarah? And don't lie to me. Whom do you work for?"

"Did you really think they were going to let you walk away without any kind of protection after what happened, Damon?" Sarah kept the sympathy from her voice, knowing it would only anger him further.

He swore bitterly. "I told them I wasn't going to be responsible for another death. Get the hell off my property,

Sarah, and don't you come back." Something deep inside of him unexpectedly hurt like hell. He had just met her. The hope hadn't even fully developed, only in his heart, not his mind, but he still felt it. It was a betrayal and his Sarah, mysterious Sarah with her beautiful smile and her lying eyes, had broken him before he'd even managed to find himself.

"I can assure you, Mr. Wilder, despite the fact that I'm a woman, I'm very capable of doing my job." Deliberately she tried to refocus the argument, putting stiff outrage in her tone.

"I don't care how good you are at your damned job or anything else. Get off my property before I call the sheriff and have you arrested for trespassing." Damon slammed the window closed with a terrible finality. The light went off as if somehow that would cut all communication between them.

Sarah sat on the ground and stared at the darkened window with a heavy heart. The sea rolled and boomed with a steadiness that never ceased. The wind tugged at her hair and the clouds drifted above her head. She drew up her knees and contemplated the fact that old prophecies should never be passed from generation to generation. That way, one could never be disappointed.

Chapter 4

SARAH DIDN'T BOTHER to knock politely on the locked
door. Damon Wilder was hurt and angry and she didn't really
blame him. She was nearly as confused as he was. Curses on
old prophecies that insisted on messing up lives. If they'd been
two people meeting casually everything would have been all
right. But no, the gate had to stand open in welcome. It was
neither of their faults, but how was she going to explain a two-
hundred-year-old foretelling? How was she going to tell him
her family came from a long line of powerful women who
drew power from the universe around them and that prophecies
several hundreds of years old *always* came true?

Sarah did the only thing any self-respecting woman would
do in the middle of the night. She pulled out her small set of
tools and picked the front door lock. She made a mental note
to install a decent security system in his house and lecture him
about at least buying a dead bolt in the interim.

As a child she had often played in the house and she knew
its layout almost as well as she knew her own. Sarah moved
swiftly through the living room. She saw very little furniture
although Damon had moved in well over a month earlier. No

pictures were on the wall, nothing to indicate it was a home, not just a temporary place to dwell.

Damon lay on his bed staring up at the ceiling. He had started out seething, but there was too much fear to sustain it. Sarah had nearly walked into an ambush. It didn't matter that she had been sent to be his watchdog, she could have been killed. It didn't bear thinking about. Sarah. Shrouded in mystery. How could he fixate on a woman so quickly when he rarely noticed anyone? If he closed his eyes he could see her. There was a softness about her, a femininity that appealed to him on every level. She would probably laugh if she knew he had an unreasonable and totally mad desire to protect her.

Damon bit out another quiet oath, not certain he could force himself to pick up and leave again. Where could he go? This was the end of the earth and yet somehow they had found him after all these months. No one would be safe around him.

"Do you always lie in the dark on your bed and swear at the ceiling?" Sarah asked quietly. "Because that could become a real issue later on in our relationship."

Damon opened his eyes to stare up at her. Sarah. Real. In his bedroom dressed in a skintight black suit that clung to every curve. His mouth watered and every cell in his body leapt to life in reaction. "It happens at those times I've been betrayed. I don't know, really, a knee-jerk reaction I can't seem to stop."

Sarah looked around for a chair, couldn't find one, and shoved his legs over to make room on the bed. "Betrayal can be painful. In all honesty I haven't had the experience. My sisters guard my back, so to speak." She turned the full power of huge blue eyes on him. "Do you believe that having friends insist on your protection is a betrayal?"

He could hear the sincerity in her voice. "You don't understand." How could she? How could anyone? "They had no right to hire you, Sarah. I quit my job, retired, if you want it neat and tidy. I have no intention of ever going back again. I cut all ties with that job and every branch of the military and the private sector."

"You tried to keep everyone around you safe by leaving." It was a statement of fact. He would think she was crazy if she told him he carried Death with him. "What happened, Damon?"

"Didn't they give you a three-inch-thick file to read on me before they sent you here?" he demanded, trying to sustain his anger with her.

Sarah simply waited, allowing the silence to lengthen and stretch between them. Sometimes silence was more eloquent than words. Damon was tense, his body rigid next to hers. His fingers were curled into a tight fist around the comforter. Sarah laid her hand gently over his.

He could have resisted most anything, but not that silent gesture of camaraderie. He twisted his hand around until his fingers laced through hers. "They hit us about five blocks from work. Dan Treadway was with me. We planned to have dinner and go back to work. We both wanted to see if we could work out a glitch with a minor problem we were having with the project." He chose his words carefully. He no longer worked for the government but his work had been classified.

"They beat us both nearly unconscious before they threw us in the trunk. They didn't even pretend to want our money. They drove to a warehouse, an old paint factory, and demanded information on a project we just couldn't safely give them."

Sarah felt his hand tremble in hers. She had read the hospital report. Both men had been tortured. She knew Damon carried the scars from numerous burns on his torso. "I couldn't give them what they wanted and poor Dan had no idea what they were even talking about." He pressed his fingertips to his eyes as if the pressure would stop the pain. Stop the memory that never left him. "He never even worked on the project they wanted information about."

Sarah knew Dan Treadway had been shot in the knee and then again in the head, killing him. Damon had refused to turn over classified information that could have resulted in the deaths of several field agents. And he had steadfastly refused to give up the newest defense system. Damon started a fire with paint thinners, nearly blowing up the building. In his escape attempt he was crushed between the wall of the warehouse and the grille of a car, severely damaging his hip and leg.

"I don't want friends, Sarah. No one can afford to be my friend."

Sarah knew he spoke the truth. Death clung and searched

for victims. She wouldn't tell him, but often Death felt cheated. If that were the case, it would demand a sacrifice before it would be appeased. "Does the company know who these people are?" Sarah prompted.

His dark gaze was haunted. "You would know that better than I would. Enemies of our country. Mercenaries. Hell, who cares? They wanted something my brain conceived, bad enough to kill an innocent man for it. I don't want to think up anything worth killing over again. So here I am."

"Did you talk to anyone, a doctor?"

He laughed. "Of course I did. The company made certain I talked to one, especially after I announced my retirement. There were a few loose ends and they didn't want me leaving. I didn't much care what they wanted." He turned his head. Edgy. Brooding. "Is it part of your job to try to get me to go back?"

Sarah shook her head. "I don't tell people what to do, Damon. I don't believe in that." Her mouth curved. "Well," she hedged, "I guess that's not altogether true. There is the exception of my sisters. They expect me to boss them around, though, because I'm the oldest and I'm very good at bossing."

"Did you want to come back here, Sarah?" The sound of the sea was soothing. It did sound like home.

"More than anything. I've felt the pull of the ocean for a while now. I've always known I'd come back home and settle here. I just don't know when I'm going to manage it. Damon, your house has no security whatsoever. Did it occur to you they could waltz in here and grab you again?"

Damon tried not to read too much into that worried note in her voice. Tried not to think that it was personal. "It's been months. I thought they would leave me alone."

Sarah whistled softly. "You even lie with that straight face and those angelic eyes. I'm taking notes. That one is right up there with swearing at the ceiling. You wanted them to come after you, didn't you?" It was a shrewd guess. She hadn't known him long enough to judge his character yet, but she'd read the files thoroughly and every word portrayed a relentless, tenacious man, focused on his goals at all times.

"Wouldn't you? They forced me to make a choice between information that is vital to our nation and my friend's life. He was looking at me when they shot him, Sarah. I'll never forget the way he looked at me." He rubbed his throbbing temple. The vision haunted his dreams and brought him out of a sound sleep so that he sat up, heart pounding, screaming a denial to the uncaring night.

"What kind of a plan do you have?"

Damon felt his stomach knot up. Her tone was very interested. She expected a plan. He had the reputation of being a brain. He should have a plan. His plan had been to draw his enemies to him and dispose of them, first with his cane and then he'd call the sheriff. He doubted if Sarah would be impressed.

She sighed. "Damon, tell me you did have a plan."

"Just because you walk on water doesn't mean everyone else does," he muttered.

"Who told you I walked on water?" Sarah demanded, annoyed. "For heaven's sake, I only did it once and it was just showing off. All my sisters can do the same thing."

He gaped at her, his eyes wide with shock. She kept a straight face, but the laughter in her eyes gave her away. Damon did the noble thing and shoved her off the bed. Sarah landed on the floor, her soft laughter inviting him to join in.

"You so deserved that," she said. "You really did. Walk on water. That's a new one. Where did you hear that? And you believed it, too."

Damon turned on his side, propped up on one elbow to look down at her. "I started the rumor myself at Inez's store. For a minute there I thought I was psychic."

"Oh, thank you so much; now all the kids will be asking me to show them. The next time you come calling I'm going to sic the dogs on you."

"What makes you think I'm going to come calling?" he asked curiously.

"I never told you about the paint preservative. You're a persistent man." She leaned her head against the bed. "Do you have a family anywhere, Damon?"

"I was an only child. My parents died years ago, first my father, then six months later my mother. They were wild about each other."

"How strange that would be, to grow up alone. I've had my sisters always and can't imagine life without them."

His fingers crept of their own accord to find the thick mass of her hair. She was wearing it in a tight braid, but he managed to rub the silky strands between his thumb and finger. How the hell did she manage to get her hair so soft? Mysterious Sarah. He was fast beginning to think of her as *his* Sarah. "Do you like them all?"

Sarah smiled there in the darkness. She loved her sisters. There was no question about that, but no one had ever thought to ask if she liked them. "Very much, Damon. You would, too. Each of them is unique and gifted in her own way. All of them have a great sense of humor. We laugh a lot at our house." He was tugging at her hair. It didn't hurt, in fact it was a pleasant sensation, but it was causing little butterfly wings to flutter in the pit of her stomach. "What are you doing?"

"I snagged my watch in your braid and thought I'd just take it out," he answered casually. He was lying and he didn't even care that it was a lie and that she knew it was a lie. Any excuse to see her hair tumbling down in a cloud around her face.

Sarah laughed softly. "My braid? Or your watch?" He was definitely tugging her hair out of its tight arrangement. "It took me twenty minutes to get my hair like that. I've never been good at hair things."

"A wasted twenty minutes. You have beautiful hair. There's no need to be good at hair things."

Sarah was absurdly pleased that he'd noticed. It was her one call to glory. "Thank you." She tapped her fingers on her knee, trying to find a way to get him to agree with her on his protection. "Damon, it's important to protect your house. I could set up a good security system for you. I'll let the sheriff know we have a problem and they'll help us out."

"Us? Sarah, you need to be as far away from me as possible." Even as he said it, his hands were tunneling in the rich wealth of her hair, a hopeless compulsion he couldn't prevent. He wanted to feel that silky softness sliding over his skin.

"I thought you were supposed to be brilliant, Damon. Didn't I read in your file that you were one of the smartest men on the face of the earth? Along with your swearing issues and your hair issues, please tell me you don't have idiot macho tendencies, too. If that's the case, I'm going to have to seriously study this gate prophecy. I can live with the other things but idiocy might be stretching my patience."

He tugged on her hair to make certain she was paying attention. "*One* of the smartest men? Is that what that report said? I should read the file over for you and weed out the blatant lies. I'm certain I'm *the* smartest, not *one* of the smartest. You don't have to insult me by pretending the report said otherwise. And what is the gate prophecy?"

She waved away his inquiry. "I'll have to tell you about the Drake history sometime, but right now, I think you might clear up the idiot macho issue for me," she insisted. "Brainy men tend to be arrogant but they shouldn't be stupid. I'm a security expert, Damon."

He sighed loudly. "So I'm supposed to tell all my friends that my lady friend is the muscle in our relationship."

"Do we have a relationship?" She tilted her head to look back at him. "And surely the smartest man on earth would have a strong enough ego to be fine with his lady friend being the muscle. Relationship or no."

"Oh, if there's no relationship, I doubt if any man could take that big a blow to his ego, Sarah. We need to call in an expert on this subject, consult a counselor before we make a decision. And it never hurts to get a second opinion if we don't like the first one."

Damon couldn't help the grin that spread across his face. It felt good to smile. She had thrown his life into complete confusion, but she made him smile. Made him want to laugh. Intrigued him. Turned him inside out. Gave him a reason to live. And the heavy weight that seemed to be pressing down on his shoulders and chest was lifted for just a few moments.

"You won't have to worry on that score, Damon. We'll have six very loud and long-winded second opinions. My sisters will have more to say than you'll ever want to hear on the subject. For that matter, on every subject. You won't need a counselor for anything; they'll all be happy to oblige, absolutely free of charge."

Sarah glanced toward the cliff house. Through the bedroom window that should have had the drapes closed. The curtains were parted in the middle, pushed to either side by an unseen hand.

"Sarah." There was an ache in Damon's voice.

Her heart did a funny little jump in her chest and she turned her head to look at him. Her gaze collided with his. Stark hunger was in his eyes. Raw need. Desire. He reached for her, caught the nape of her neck, and slowly lowered his head to hers. His mouth fastened onto hers. They simply melted together. Merged.

Fireworks might have burst in the air around them. Or maybe it was the stars scattering across the sky, glittering like gems. Fire raced up her skin, heat spread through her body. He claimed her. Branded her. And he did a thorough job of it. They fed on one another. Were lost in smoky desire. His mouth was perfect, hot and hungry and demanding and possessive.

No one had ever kissed her like that. She had never thought it would be like that. She wanted to just stay there all night and kiss.

Damon shifted his weight on the bed, deepening the kiss. He tumbled over the edge, sprawling on the floor, pulling her over so that she collapsed on top of him. Instantly his arms circled her and held her to his chest.

Sarah could feel the laughter start deep inside him, where it started in her. They lay in a tangle of arms and legs, laughing happily. She lifted her head to look at him, to trace his wonderful mouth with her fingertip. "Sheer magic, Damon. That's what you are. Does this happen every time you kiss a woman?"

"I don't kiss women," he admitted, shaken to his very core. His fingers were tunneling in her wealth of hair, her thick silky hair that he wanted to bury his face in.

"Well, men then. Does it happen all the time? Because quite frankly it's amazing. You're truly amazing."

The laughter welled up all over again. Damon helped her to sit up, her back against the bed. He sat next to her. Both of them stared out the window toward the cliff house.

"I could have sworn I closed those drapes," he commented.

"You probably did," Sarah admitted with a small sigh. "It's the sisters. My sisters. They're probably watching us right this minute. Hannah came home right before I left and Kate and Abigail arrived about the time the driver was shooting at me. You could wave at them if you felt up to it."

"How are they watching us?" Damon asked, interested.

"The telescope. I use it to watch the sky." She used her most pious voice. "And sometimes the ocean, but my sisters are notoriously and pathetically interested in *my* business. I shall have to teach them some manners.' She waved her hand casually, murmuring something he couldn't quite catch, but it sounded light and airy and melodious.

Shadows entered the room. Moved. The drapes swayed gently, blocked the sliver of moon, the faint light reflected by the pounding sea. Damon blinked; in that split second the curtains were drawn firmly across the window.

Chapter 5

"YOU WERE KISSING that man," Hannah accused gleefully. "Sarah Drake, you hussy. You were kissing a perfect stranger."

Sarah looked as cool as possible under fire. "I don't know what you thought you saw with your eye glued to the telescope lens, but certainly not that! You ought to be ashamed of yourself spying that way. And using . . ." She trailed off to motion in the air with her fingers, glaring at all three of her sisters as she did so. "To open the curtains in a private bedroom is an absolute no-no, which we all agreed on when we set down the rules."

"There are exceptions to the rules," Kate pointed out demurely. She was curled up in a straight-backed wooden chair at the table, her knees drawn up, with a wide, engaging grin on her face as she painted her toenails.

"What exceptions?" Sarah demanded, her hands on her hips.

Kate shrugged and blew on her toenails before answering. "When our sister is hanging out with a man with a black aura around him." She raised her head to look at Sarah, her gaze steady. "That's very dangerous and you know it. You can't play around with Death. Not even you, Sarah."

Sarah turned to glare at Hannah. She didn't want to talk about it, or even name Death, afraid if she gave it substance she would increase its power, so she remained silent.

Hannah shook her head. "It wasn't me ratting you out. You left the tea leaves in the cup and it was there for everyone to read."

"You still had no right to go against the rules without a vote." Sarah was fairly certain she'd lost the argument, but she wasn't going down without a fight. They were right about Death. Just the idea of facing it made her shiver inside. If she wasn't so drawn to Damon, she would have backed away and allowed nature to take its course. For some unexplained reason, she couldn't bear the thought of Damon suffering.

Kate smirked. "Don't worry, we made certain to convene a hasty meeting and vote on whether or not the situation called for the use of power. It was fully agreed upon that it was wholly warranted."

"You convened a meeting?" Sarah glared at them all with righteous indignation. "Without me? Without the others? The three of you don't make up the majority. Oh, you are in so much trouble!" she said triumphantly.

Hannah blew her a kiss, sweetly reasonable. "Of course we didn't do that, Sarah. We contacted everyone on the spot. It was perfectly legit. We told them about the gate and how it opened on its own for him. And how the dogs greeted him. Elle sent hugs and kisses and says she misses you. Joley wanted to come home right away and get in on the fun but she's tied up." She frowned. "I hope not literally, I didn't think to ask and you never know with Joley. And Libby is working in Guatemala or some other place she's discovered with no bathroom and probably leeches, healing the sick children as usual."

"I thought she was in Africa investigating that crawlie thing that was killing everyone when they tried to harvest their crops," Kate said. "She was sending me some research material for my next book."

"Wherever she is, Libby agreed totally we needed to make certain Sarah was safe." Hannah looked innocent. "That's all we were doing, Sarah. Everyone agreed that for your safety we needed to see into that bedroom immediately."

Kate and Abbey burst into laughter again. "I was a bit worried when he got so exuberant he fell on the floor," Abbey said. "But clearly you weren't in a life-threatening situation so we left you to it."

"And boy, did you go to it," Kate added. "Really, Sarah, a little less enthusiasm on your part might have gone a long way toward giving some credence to our chasing-men theory." The three sisters exchanged nods as if research were very important.

Struggling not to laugh, Sarah tapped her foot, hands on hips, looking at their unrepentant faces. "You knew I wasn't in any danger, you peeping Thomasinas. Shame on the lot of you! I'll have you know I was *working* last night."

That brought another round of laughter that nearly tipped Kate right out of the chair. "A *working* girl!"

"Is that what you call it? You were working at *something,* Sarah," Hannah agreed.

"She's a *fast* worker," Abbey added.

Sarah's mouth twitched with the effort to remain straight-faced. "I do security work, you horrible hags. I'm his bodyguard!"

Kate did fall off the chair laughing. Hannah slumped over the table, her elegant body gracefully posed. "You were guarding his body all right, Sarah," Abbey said, just managing to get the words out through the shrieks of laughter.

"*Closely* guarding his body," Kate contributed.

"Locked up those lips nice and safe," Hannah agreed. "Ooh, Sarah, baby, you are *great* at that job."

Sarah's only recourse was to fall back on dignity. They weren't listening to their big sister's voice of *total authority* at their antics. She drew herself up, looked as haughty as she could with the three of them rolling around together, laughing like hyenas. "Go ahead and howl, but the three of you just might want to read that old prophecy. Read the *entire* thing, not just the first line or two."

The smile faded from Hannah's face. "Sarah's looking awfully smug. Where is that old book anyway?"

Abbey sat up straight. "Sarah Drake, you didn't dare cast on us, did you?"

"I don't cast," Sarah said, "that's Hannah's department. Damon is coming over. I wanted him to meet you." She looked suddenly vulnerable. "I really like him. We talked all night about everything. You know those uncomfortable silences with strangers who can't possibly understand us? We didn't have one of them. He's so worn out from carrying Death. Of course, he doesn't know that's what he's doing and if he did, he would have sent me away immediately."

"Oh, Sarah." Hannah's voice was filled with compassion.

"I have to find a way to help him. He couldn't bear another death on his hands. His friend was killed, but he managed to save himself." She swept a hand through her hair and looked at her sisters with desperation in her eyes. "I liked everything about him. There wasn't a subject we skipped. And we laughed together over everything." She lifted her gaze to her sisters. "I really, really liked him."

"Then we'll like him, too," Kate reassured her. "And we'll find a way to help him." She opened the refrigerator and peered in, pulling at drawers. "Did you get fresh veggies?"

"Of course, and plenty of fruit. By the way, congratulations on your latest release. I read it cover to cover and it was wonderful. As always, Katie, your stories are fantastic," Sarah praised sincerely. "And thanks, Kate."

Abbey hugged Kate. "My favorite memories are when we were little and we used to lie on the balcony looking up at the stars, with you telling us your stories. You deserve all those bestseller lists."

Kate kissed her sister. "And you aren't prejudiced at all."

"Even if we were," Hannah said, "you're still the best storyteller ever born and deserve every award and list you get on."

Kate blushed, turning nearly as red as the highlights in her chestnut hair. She looked pleased. "How did the spotlight get turned on me? Sarah's the one who spent the night with a perfect stranger."

"I had to spend the night with him," Sarah insisted. "There's no security at his house. And I've asked Jonas Harrington to drop by this morning to meet Damon."

All three women groaned in unison. "How could you invite that Neanderthal to our home, Sarah?" Hannah demanded.

"He's the local sheriff," Sarah pointed out. "Come on, all that was a long time ago—we were kids."

"He was a total jerk to me and he still is," Hannah said.

The mug, filled with coffee, on the table in front of her began to steam. Hannah looked down and saw the liquid was beginning to boil. Hastily she blew on the surface.

There was a small silence. "Fine!" Hannah exploded. "I'll admit he still makes me mad if I just think about him. And if he calls me Baby Doll or Barbie Doll, I'm turning him into a big fat toad. He already is one, he may as well look like it."

"You can't turn the sheriff into a toad, Hannah. It's against the rules," Abbey reminded her. "Give him a doughnut gut or a nervous twitch."

"That's not good enough," Kate chimed in. "You need imagination to pay that man back. Something much more subtle—like every time he goes to lie to a woman to get her in bed, he blurts out the truth or tells them what a hound dog he is."

"I'll do worse than that," Hannah threatened, "I'll make it so he's lousy in bed! Mister Macho Man, the bad boy who couldn't do anything but make fun of me in school. He thinks he's such a lady's man."

"Hannah." Sarah heard the pain in her sister's voice and spoke gently. "You were then, and still are now, so incredibly beautiful and brainy. No one could ever conceive of you being so painfully shy. You hid it well. No one knew you threw up before school every day or that we had to work combined spells to keep you functioning in public situations. They wouldn't know you still have problems. You've faced those fears by doing the things that terrify you and you're always successful. Outsiders see your beauty and brains and success. They don't see what you're hiding in private."

"Someone's coming up the path," Kate said without looking away from Hannah. She held out her hand to her sister. "We're all so proud of you, Hannah. Who cares what Jonas Harrington thinks?"

"It's not Harrington, although he's close by somewhere," Abbey said. "I think it's Sarah's gate crasher. You know, the one she spent the night with. I still can't get over that, and Elle says she wants every intimate detail the minute you get a chance."

"There are no intimate details," Sarah objected, exasperated. "I'm going to install a security system for him. Kate, don't let them read your books anymore, you're giving them wild imaginations."

"It wasn't our imaginations that he was kissing you," Hannah pointed out gleefully. "We *saw* you!"

"And you were kissing him back," Abbey added.

"Well, that part wasn't altogether my fault!" Sarah defended. "He's a *great* kisser. What could I do but kiss the man back?"

The sisters looked at one another solemnly and burst out laughing simultaneously. The dog curled up in the corner lifted his head and whined softly to get their attention.

"He's here, Sarah, and the gate must have opened for him a second time," Kate said, intrigued. "I really have to take a long look at the Drake history book. I want to see *exactly* what that prophecy says. How strange that something written hundreds of years ago applies to us even in this modern day and age."

"Kate, sweetie," Abbey said, "every age thinks it's progressive and modern but in reality we're going to be considered backward someday."

"He's on the verandah," Kate announced and hurried to the front door.

Her sisters trailed after her. Sarah's heart began to race. Damon was not the kind of man she had ever considered she'd be attracted to, yet she couldn't stop thinking about him. She thought a lot about his smile, the way two small dents appeared near the corners of his mouth. Intriguing, tempting little dents. He had the kind of smile that invited long drugging kisses, hot, melting together. . . .

"Sarah!" Hannah hissed her name. "The temperature just went up a hundred degrees in here. You know you can't think like that around us. Sheesh! One day with this man and your entire moral code has collapsed."

Sarah considered arguing, but she didn't have much of a defense. If Damon hadn't been such a gentleman and stopped at just kissing, she might have made love to him. All right, she *would* have made love to him. She *should* have made love to him. She lay awake all night, hot and bothered and edgy with need. Darn the man for having chivalrous manners anyway. She smiled and touched her mouth with a feeling of awe.

He had kissed her most of the night. Delicious, wonderful, sinfully rich kisses . . .

"Sarah!" All three of her sisters reprimanded her at once.

Sarah grinned at them unrepentantly. "I can't help it, he just affects me that way."

"Well, try not to throw yourself at him," Abbey urged. "It's so unbecoming in a Drake. Dignity at all times when it comes to men."

Hannah was looking out the window. She wrinkled her nose. "Kate, when you open the door for Damon, do let the dogs out for their morning romp. They've been cooped up all night, the poor things."

Kate nodded and obediently waved the dogs through as she greeted Damon. "How nice to see you, Mr. Wilder. Sarah has told us so much about you."

The dogs rushed past Damon. He leaned heavily on his cane, watching the large animals charge the sheriff, who was making his way up the path. Just as the man reached the gate, it swung closed with a loud bang. The dogs hit it hard, growling, baring their teeth, and digging frantically in an effort to get at their prey.

"This isn't funny, Hannah!" Jonas Harrington yelled. "I was *invited* by your sister and I showed up as a favor. Stop being so childish and call off your hounds."

Hannah smiled sweetly at Damon and held out her hand. "Pay no attention to the toad, Mr. Wilder, he comes around every now and then playing with his little gun, thinking he's going to impress the natives." She yawned, covering her mouth delicately. "It's so boring and childish but we have to humor him."

Sarah whistled sharply and the dogs instantly ceased growling, backing away from the fence to return to the house. When the animals were safely by her side, the gate swung open invitingly and the sheriff stalked through, his face a grim mask, his slashing gaze fixed on Hannah.

"What happens if you don't humor him?" Damon asked.

"Why, he throws his power around harassing us with tickets for speeding," Hannah said, holding her ground, her chin up.

"You *were* speeding, Hannah. Did you think I was going to let you off just because you're beautiful?" The sheriff shook hands with Damon. "Jonas Harrington, the only sane one when it comes to Baby Doll's true character."

Hannah flashed him a brilliant smile. Her sisters moved closer to her, protectively, Damon thought. "Why not, Sheriff? All the other cops *always* let me off." She turned on her heel and walked away.

Kate and Abbey let out a collective soft sigh.

"You gave my sister a ticket?" Sarah asked, outraged. "Jonas, you really are a self-centered toad. Why can't you just leave her alone? It's so high school to keep up grudges. Get over it."

"She was the one speeding like a teenager," Jonas pointed out. "Aside from feeding me to your dogs, did you have a real reason for inviting me up here?"

Taunting laughter floated back to them. "Don't flatter yourself, Harrington; nobody *wants* you here."

As Jonas Harrington stepped into the house, the ivy hanging from the ceiling swayed precariously and a thick ropy vine slapped him in the back of his head. Jonas spun around, his hands up as if to fight. He shoved the plant away from him and stormed into the living room, muttering foul curses beneath his breath.

Damon was behind him and stopped immediately, looking warily around the room, then back to the ivy. "Do your plants eat your visitors often?" he asked with grave curiosity as he pushed the vine away from him with his cane. Gingerly he walked around the masses of greenery.

"Only the ones who are mean to my sisters," Sarah replied.

Without warning, startling both of them, Damon suddenly reached out, caught Sarah by the nape of her neck, and dragged her to him. His mouth fastened on hers hungrily. Sarah melted into him. Merged. Became liquid fire. Went up in flames. Her arms crept around his neck. The cane dropped on the floor and they were devouring each other. The world fell away until there was only Damon and Sarah and raging need.

"Sarah!" The name shimmered in the air, breaking them apart so that they just stood, clinging, staring into each other's eyes, drowning. Shocked.

Sarah blinked, trying to focus, then looked around and blushed when she saw Jonas Harrington gaping. "Close your mouth, Jonas," she commanded, her tone daring him to make a comment. She'd known Jonas all of her life. Of course he couldn't pass up the opportunity. She waited, cringing.

"Holy smoke." Jonas held out his hand to Damon. "You're a god. Kissing a Drake woman is dangerous, kind of like taking a chance on kissing a viper. You just dove right in and went for it." He pumped Damon's hand with great enthusiasm.

"Ha ha." Sarah glared at the sheriff. "Don't you start, and don't you spread any rumors either, Jonas. I'm already annoyed with you for giving Hannah a ticket."

The smile faded from the sheriff's face. "I don't think because a woman is drop-dead gorgeous she should be treated any differently. She has everything too easy, Sarah. You all treat her like a little baby doll."

"You don't know Hannah at all, Jonas, and you don't deserve to know her. She wouldn't expect you to let her slide because of her looks, you idiot." Sarah threw her hands into the air. "Forget it, I'm finished trying to explain anything to you. If you don't understand friendship by now you never will. Let's get on with this. Damon and I have a busy schedule today." She gestured toward a chair.

Harrington was looking toward the stairs.

"Sit!" Sarah demanded. "This is business. Murder. Right up your alley, Jonas."

Chapter 6

JONAS HARRINGTON LISTENED calmly while Sarah told him the events that had taken place the night before. His dark features hardened perceptibly while she talked. He flicked a smoldering glare toward Kate and Abbey. "Why wasn't I called last night? I might have been able to do something last night. Damn it, Sarah, where's your head? You could have been killed!"

"Well, I wasn't. I saved the rifle for you, hoping you might get prints off of it, but I doubt it." Sarah smiled at him.

Jonas shook his head. "Don't do that; you've been giving me that same smile since kindergarten and it always gets you out of trouble." He gestured toward her face. "Take a long look at her, Damon, because that's going to be her answer every time she does something you don't like." He leaned forward in his chair, his eyes slashing at her. "What about your sisters? Did it even occur to you that you might bring these people down on your own house?"

Furious, he rose, a big man, moving like a jungle cat, pacing restlessly through the long living room. "These men are professionals. You both know that. Whatever you did to bring this on . . ."

"He worked in a high-security job, Jonas, nothing illegal. It isn't drug related so get that right out of your head."

Damon leaned back in his chair, torn between worry that he'd placed the Drake family in danger and feeling pleased that Sarah had turned protective. She immediately had become a fierce tigress ready to spring if the sheriff continued to cast aspersions on his character.

"I want to know what we're up against. And don't start throwing words around like security clearance to me. If we have a couple of men willing to break into a house with a high-powered rifle—"

"They had a tranq dart in it," Sarah interrupted hastily.

"I was kidnapped, along with my assistant, nearly a year ago. My assistant was killed and I barely escaped with my life." As Damon spoke, a dark shadow fell across the room. Outside, the ocean waves thundered and sprayed into the air. "They wanted information that could have affected the security of our nation and I refused to give it to them." Damon passed a hand over his face as if wiping away a nightmare. "I know that sounds melodramatic, but . . ." He slowly unbuttoned his shirt to expose his chest and the whorls and scars left behind. "I want you to know what these people are like."

The shadow lengthened and grew along the wall behind Damon. The shadow began to take shape, gray, translucent, but there all the same, growing in form until a faceless ghoul emerged with outstretched arms and a long thin body. The mouth yawned open wide, a gesture of greed and craving for the addiction Death had developed. The arms could have been reaching for either Jonas or Damon.

Damon hunched away from Jonas, pain flickering across his face, his shoulders stiffening as if under a great load.

Alarmed, Hannah reached out and jerked Jonas halfway across the room out of harm's way. Jonas swore under his breath and planted his feet firmly, thinking she was attempting to throw him out of the house.

Sarah adjusted the blinds at the window, filtering out the light, and returned to Damon's side, touching him gently. That was all. The lightest of touches. She simply laid her hand over his, yet peace stole into him as he buttoned his shirt. The terrible weight that always seemed to be pressing him into the ground lightened.

Kate's eyes filled with tears and she pressed her fingers to her mouth.

Abbey left the room to return with a cup of tea. "Drink this, Damon," she said. "You'll enjoy the taste."

The aroma alone added to the soothing touch Sarah had provided. He didn't think to ask how she had managed to make hot tea in a matter of seconds.

"I could use a cup of tea," Jonas said, "if anyone's asking. And a touch of sanity in the house would be nice, too. Baby Doll was going to huck me right out the door and you all just stood there watching."

"I'll make it for you." Hannah leaned against the door frame and looked up at the sheriff. Her fingers twisted together, the only sign of her agitation. "Do you like it sweet? I'm certain I can come up with an appropriate concoction."

"I think I'll pass altogether. One of these days I'm going to retaliate, Hannah."

She made a face at him as he crossed to the sliding-glass door to stare outside at the pounding waves. "I have a bad feeling about this, Sarah. I know you're used to doing things differently and people have no idea how you do it. Maybe you don't know either, I certainly don't, but I believe in you. I sometimes just feel things. It's one of the things that makes me good at my job." He turned to look at her. "I have a *very* bad feeling about this. Frankly, I'm afraid for all of you."

There was a small silence. "I believe you, Jonas," Sarah said. "I've always known you had a gift."

His gaze moved around the room, restlessly touching on each woman. "I've known this family since I was a boy. Feuds"—his smoldering gaze went to Hannah—"are petty when it comes to your safety. I'm not losing any of you over this. I want to be called if one of you stubs your toe. If you see a stranger or you hear a funny noise. I'm not kidding around with you over this issue. I want your word that you'll call me. You have my private number as well as the number to the office and 911."

"Jonas, don't worry, we'll be fine. I'm very good at what I do," Sarah said with complete confidence.

Jonas took a step toward her, very reminiscent of a stalking panther. Damon was grateful he was too old to be intimidated. "I want your word. Every one of you."

Damon nodded. "I have to agree with Harrington. These men tortured us. They don't play around. I'll admit when I'm around you, I feel magic in the air, but these men are evil and capable of torture and murder. I have to know you're all safe or I'll have to leave this town."

"Damon!" Sarah looked stricken. "They'll just follow you." Worse, he would carry Death with him wherever he chose to go.

"Then cooperate with the sheriff. Give him whatever he needs to stop these men." As ridiculous as it seemed when he'd just met her, Damon couldn't bear the thought of leaving Sarah, but he wasn't about to risk her life.

"I don't mind calling you, Jonas," Kate said readily.

Abbey held up her hand. "I'm in."

Sarah nodded. "I'm always grateful for help from the local law."

All eyes turned to Hannah. She shrugged indifferently. "Whatever helps Damon, I'm willing to do."

Jonas ignored the grudge in her voice and nodded. "I want all of you to watch your step. Be aware of your surroundings and any strangers. Keep those dogs close and lock up the house!"

"We're all over it," Sarah agreed. "Really, Jonas, we don't want any part of men with guns. We'll call you even if the cat meows."

He looked a little mollified. "I'll want extra patrols around here as well as around Damon's house, Sarah."

"Well, of course, Jonas," Sarah agreed.

"It will give me every opportunity to make friends with them," Hannah said. "I don't know many of the new people in town."

Jonas glared at her. "You and your slinky body can just stay away from my deputies."

Hannah made a face at him, raised her hand to push at the hair spilling across her face. An icy wind rushed through the room, giving life to the curtains, so that they danced in a macabre fashion, fluttering, reaching toward Jonas as if to bind him in the thick folds.

Sarah glimpsed a dark shadow moving within the drapes. Her hands went up in a casual, graceful wave. Kate and Abbey followed the gentle movements with their own. The wind died abruptly and the curtains dropped into place.

Damon cleared his throat. "Does someone want to tell me what happened?"

Jonas shook his head. "Never be dumb enough to ask for an explanation from any of them, Damon. You might get it and your hair will turn gray." His gaze swung to Hannah. "Don't even think about it. Ladies, I can find my own way out."

Damon didn't take his eyes from Sarah. She was looking at Hannah and there was accusation in her gaze. Out of the corner of his eye, he could see Abbey and Kate doing the same thing.

Hannah threw her hands into the air. "I wasn't thinking, okay? I'm sorry."

The silence lengthened, disapproval thick in the room.

Hannah sighed. "I really am sorry. I forgot for just a moment about Dea—" She broke off abruptly, her gaze shifting to Damon. "About the other thing we're dealing with. It won't happen again."

"It better not," Sarah said. "You can't afford to forget for one moment. This is too dangerous, Hannah."

"Wait a minute," Damon interrupted. "If you're talking about me and those men the other night, I don't want your family involved in any way."

"The men?" Kate raised her eyebrow. "Not in the least, Damon, didn't give them a thought. There are things far more dangerous than human beings."

He watched the four women exchange long knowing looks and was exasperated. They knew something he didn't. Something regarding him. "I can understand why poor Harrington gets so frustrated with you."

Sarah rose and blew him a kiss. "He loves all seven of us. He just likes to puff out his chest."

"He was genuinely worried," Damon said. "And I am, too. The things he said make sense. It's bad enough to think of you in danger, let alone all your sisters." He raked a hand through his hair in agitation. "I can't be responsible for that."

To his shock they all laughed. "Damon." Sarah's voice was a mixture of amusement and tenderness. "We accepted responsibility for our own decisions a very long time ago. We're grown women. When we choose to involve ourselves in problems, we accept the consequences." She leaned toward him.

Abbey groaned dramatically. "She's going to do it. She's going to kiss him right in front of us."

"That is so not fair, Sarah," Hannah protested.

"Go ahead," Kate encouraged. "I need to write a good love scene."

When Sarah hesitated, her gaze lost in his, Damon took advantage and did the job thoroughly, not wanting to let Kate down.

Chapter 7

DAMON HEARD LAUGHTER drifting up from the beach as he limped around the corner of his deck to set his teacup on the small table beside his rocking chair. His hip was bothering him more than usual and Sarah wasn't there to make it better. She'd spent the last several days dragging more and more equipment into his house, setting up a security system that might rival Fort Knox.

Jonas Harrington followed him, but instead of taking the chair Damon waved him toward, he stepped to the corner of the deck to watch the figures running barefoot in the sand on the beach far below. "They're up to something."

Damon sank into his chair where he had a great view of that small, private beach. The Drake sisters often were on it, day or night, their laughter drifting on the wind, the sound as soothing as the sea itself.

He missed Sarah. It was silly to miss someone when he saw her every single day. He'd always been a loner and it didn't make sense to him to need to see her quick, flashing smile. He especially loved to watch her eyes light up each time she saw him. He'd take the memory of that expression on her face to his grave.

"I'm beginning to think there really is something magical about the Drake family. I've never needed to be around anyone, but I can't imagine never seeing Sarah Drake again. I thought my life was my work. My brain runs a hundred miles an hour, always sorting through ideas, but she calms me. Don't ask me how." Damon could pick her out easily, her long dark hair blowing free in the wind. She often swept it up in a ponytail, her natural beauty so real to him when she thought nothing of her looks. "She doesn't think she's beautiful. Isn't that strange?"

Jonas shrugged. "I don't think any of them think about their looks all that much, other than Baby Doll. They spoil her and treat her like a little princess." He raked a hand through his hair, frowning. "Well, I shouldn't say that." His gaze remained on the tall, thin blonde with the waves of platinum hair streaming down her back. "Sometimes I think they cater to her—and other times I think they take advantage of her. Don't ask me how, it's just a feeling."

"You like them." Damon took a sip of the hot tea. He never drank tea as a rule, but Sarah had brought him a special blend from Hannah and he found it made him feel better when the weight of guilt and memories seemed to crouch heaviest on his shoulder.

"I love them," Jonas corrected. "They're family. *My* family. I take that very seriously, even if they don't. They spend all of their time getting into trouble, and I don't mean something casual, I mean something dangerous."

"Like me." Damon returned the cup to the saucer and sighed. "Sarah won't back off. She took the job of guarding me and nothing I say will stop her. I've thought a hundred times about leaving so she'd be safe, but . . ." He trailed off, wishing he were a bigger man. He'd never had anyone look at him the way Sarah did and he just couldn't quite make himself give that up.

"She'd just follow you, Damon," Jonas said. "The Drakes are tenacious. Once they sink their teeth into a problem, it gets resolved, because they don't know the meaning of the word quit. Sarah won't quit you, so don't quit her."

Damon didn't flinch away from the steel in Jonas's eyes. "Don't worry, Harrington, I hear your warning. I doubt very much I can hurt Sarah, other than if my past does, but she's in danger of ripping out my heart and handing it to me on a silver platter."

"You've got it that bad?"

"Hell yes, I do. I never thought it would happen to me and in such a short time, too. I can't stop thinking about her." His mouth was dry and his heart pounding just talking about Sarah. He couldn't imagine why a woman so full of life and laughter and love would choose to be with someone so melancholy and dark. He didn't have the least bit of social skills and tended to run roughshod over people with his intellect. He rarely engaged in small, polite conversation and, in fact, knew he was rarely polite. It had never mattered before, but it mattered to Sarah.

"If it helps, I've never seen Sarah really interested in a man before. She dated some, but kept it away from the family and Sea Haven. All the girls probably have dated, but we don't see it here." Jonas frowned and turned back toward the sounds drifting on the wind, his gaze finding the tallest of the Drake sisters.

"What is up with that locked gate they all talk about?" Damon asked.

"The infamous gate." Jonas smirked. "They keep that gate padlocked at all times, like that's going to save them from something."

"Save them from what?"

Jonas shrugged. "I think love. I hear them talk sometimes, but they don't tell me much and in all honesty, I don't want to know. Their house holds generations of power. Real power. I hate talking about this stuff because it sounds too *heebie-jeebie* for me. I like to deal in facts, not magic, but you can feel the power in the house. A few years back they decided to padlock that gate and it's been kept that way ever since."

"It wasn't locked a week after Sarah came home. When I came up the path leading to the house, it was standing open. I felt like the house was welcoming me. The inscriptions on the bottom of the gate, one in Italian and one in Latin say the same thing."

"You can read Italian and Latin?" Jonas grinned at him. "No wonder Sarah's attracted to you. What does it say? I always wanted to know but wasn't about to ask them."

" 'The seven become one when united.' All the symbols

have meanings as well. Several are symbols of protection. Do they practice ancient religion?"

"Who the hell knows what they practice. They're magic and they have very real powers. Libby is a doctor and I've seen her work miracles. Abigail is a loose cannon sometimes. She utters the word 'truth' and everyone around her starts telling every secret they have. Hannah's just plain scary. Elle's very quiet and she doesn't talk much about what she can or can't do, but if she loses her temper, she could probably flatten Sea Haven. It drains them, though, to use their gifts. I've seen them to the point they can't walk or even talk. They drop in their tracks and it takes time for them to recover."

Damon looked up at the worry in the sheriff's voice. "What are you not saying to me? Why do you have that look on your face?"

Jonas nodded toward the beach. "They know something. Sarah has precog. At least I think she does. Every single morning I see her drive to your house."

"She's been working on a security system."

"I noticed. It's state of the art. But she didn't come this morning and she wasn't here this afternoon. And now it's evening and they're on the beach."

"Believe me, I know Sarah hasn't come to see me. It's all I can do not to pick up the phone and call her or go on down to that beach to see what she's up to."

"I think you should."

"Go down to the beach? I looked at the trail, Jonas. I don't think my hip will hold up."

"I'll be happy to help you."

"Why do I have the feeling you're trying to get me into big trouble with those women?"

Jonas flashed another grin. "Better you than me. The sun's going to be setting soon and they're preparing for that. The moon rising to meet the setting sun. We can make it to the small dunes and sit there and watch them up close and personal. If you want to be part of Sarah's family, you're going to have to just accept that they can do extraordinary things."

"Like walk on water?"

"I wouldn't rule it out."

"You really are a believer. I don't know that I can believe in anything I can't back up with scientific fact."

Jonas's grin grew wider. "You're in for a few shocks, Wilder. Come on, you may as well learn what the Drake family is all about."

Damon wanted to see Sarah. And he was curious about the magic they supposedly wielded. He didn't believe in voodoo and other religions that called on something he couldn't see or feel. Hell, he didn't even know if he believed in God anymore. He had the sneaking suspicion he was beginning to believe there really was something different about the Drakes. And if that were true, where did that leave him? A man of science, grounded firmly in fact.

He stood up, leaning heavily on his cane. "Hell. It would be just my luck to fall in love with a woman who can do some kind of magic. I don't even go to magic shows. I can't enjoy them until I figure out how they do what they do and then it isn't all that impressive anymore."

"Prepare to be impressed and you're not going to find a scientific answer for anything these women do. I wouldn't even bother to try, Damon, you'll just drive yourself crazy. Let's take the car as far as we can and save your leg."

"You're off duty tonight?"

Jonas nodded. "The sisters are home so I figured I might con them out of a home-cooked meal. I like to spend time with them when they're home. They rejuvenate me. Sometimes my job is disturbing. Too many accidents on the highway. The crime in Sea Haven is about nil, but the outlying areas get a bit more. For all their nonsense, the Drakes soothe me."

Damon followed him out to the car, aware, as they walked, Jonas's restless gaze was quartering the area back and forth all around them, looking for danger. Damon ducked his head. He hated that small feeling, so helpless with his damaged hip and damaged soul. He couldn't stop the nightmares and he couldn't prevent others from being in danger just because they were around him.

Jonas started the car and pulled onto the highway. "There's a small dirt road leading to the back of the Drake property. We can reach the very top of the path down to the beach from there. Steps have been dug out and most of the way down there's actually a handrail. I think you'll be safe. In any case, you'd better be or Sarah will have my hide."

"She'll probably have it anyway," Damon said.

Jonas's grin was very much in evidence. "You do know that woman, even on such short acquaintance. She can keep the others in line as well. If you're really serious about her . . ." He glanced sideways at Damon for confirmation.

"Very serious."

"Sarah doesn't put up with nonsense. She likes straight answers. She's very tolerant of people, don't get me wrong, but she's loyal and has integrity and she expects the same from the people she lets into her life."

"Thanks, Harrington," Damon said gruffly.

"For what?"

"For thinking I have a chance with her. I never expected to fall in love. Certainly not this fast. I can't tell if she's just feeling sorry for me because my life's gone down the drain, or if she's genuinely interested."

"She kissed you, Wilder. Sarah doesn't go around kissing just anyone and certainly not in front of her family."

Damon couldn't help the little spurt of happiness that seemed to ease the weight bearing down so hard on his shoulders and chest. There were some mornings when he woke up feeling as if someone was crouched on top of him. On those days, he could hardly get out of bed and only Sarah's smile brought him a semblance of peace.

This morning he had awakened with sweat pouring from his body and the dark specter of death echoing through his dreams. His shower hadn't helped lift the weight and the rest of the day had been long and difficult. He'd been grateful to see Jonas when the sheriff had stopped by to check on him. Part of Damon was afraid he was getting too used to Sarah's presence and already relying on the joy and light that always surrounded her. He brooded over the fact that she hadn't come to see him, hadn't even called him. That scared the hell out of him. He didn't look at Jonas as they drove the small distance to the driveway leading to the Drake's private beach entrance.

Jonas parked the car just above the path leading to the beach below. He stepped out and went around to help Damon. The wind touched his face gently, almost as if fingertips were caressing him, seeking his attention. The sound of the surf pounded below him and the sound of women's voices drifted up with it. He couldn't tell if they were chanting, the voices sounded rhythmic, but for some reason, he felt a chill go through his body.

As Damon stepped out of the car, a dark shadow passed overhead. Jonas glanced up, but there were no clouds, only the setting sun and the rising moon, crossing paths over the wild waves of the sea. He glanced back at Damon and his breath caught in his throat. There was a black shadow on the rising wall behind them. The dark shape appeared to be hovering over Damon, actually crouching on his shoulders. Damon bent over with the weight of the apparition, leaning heavily on his cane.

Ice cold fingers of fear frissoned down Jonas's back. The black shape took on a face, a grinning skull with skin stretched back and bony arms stretching toward Damon. Jonas stepped in front of the other man instinctively. He heard the chant swell in volume, the voices much more clear, carried on the breeze. The sky turned blood red and the boom of the sea was louder as the wind rose to a shriek, ripping and tugging at the black shape in an effort to dislodge it from Damon's shoulders.

Weight settled on Jonas and he watched the black shadow on the rock as it stretched in an effort to encompass his frame as well as Damon's.

"I can't move," Damon said. "And I'm cold all the way through my body." He hunched his shoulders against a terrible weight, his hand absently rubbing his chest, right over his heart. "What's wrong with me?"

"I don't know," Jonas said grimly. But he feared he did know. The Drake sisters were fighting for Damon's life and because he had dared to step between Damon and that shadow, they were fighting for his life as well. He felt helpless standing there with the wind blowing on his face, afraid to move, afraid the shadow would take Damon. The claws seemed stretched with greed, the head of the thing leaning toward Damon as if trying to draw the breath from his body.

The voices swelled in volume—feminine, strong, united. Not just the four on the beach, but the three other sisters reaching from distant places to join so the seven had become united as one. Jonas felt the strength and power pouring through them into him. Small glittering colors sparkled and leapt with life. Small fireworks crackled as they formed a wall between the two men and the apparition.

The shadow drew back sharply, careful to avoid the sizzling lights. Jonas felt the weight on his shoulders lessen. Damon stood a little straighter. The gray lines etched so deep in his face faded.

Jonas drew in a breath as he felt a hand brush his. He looked down, expecting to see someone beside him, gripping his fingers tightly. The sensation was there. Soft. Firm. In control. Yet no one was there. He stood alone with the wind on his face, ruffling his hair and the feel of someone holding him tightly, a feminine body pressed close to his. Everything male in him roared with protest. One of the Drakes—it felt like Hannah—shielded him, and that was just unacceptable.

He made out the shapes of several women with long flowing hair, arms raised to the sky in the midst of the crackling fireworks, insubstantial figures wavering in the air as if they were spirit rather than flesh and blood. Behind him, Damon swore softly under his breath, the actual words unintelligible, but Jonas had the same strong sense of real danger. Damon didn't want to hide behind the women any more than Jonas did.

Jonas tried to move, to step forward, to push his way through that wall of glittering lights and transparent figures to get at the crouching dark shape that was retreating slowly, driven back by the women as they pushed him away from the cliff and out toward the ocean. The soft chant was clear now, the voices strong, blending with the wind and pounding sea, filling Jonas's head with a strange kind of music.

He turned his head to follow the movement of the shadow as it took to the air, the retreat painfully slow as it moved over the sea. A whale breached and three dolphins spun in the air, spraying droplets of water in an arc over the crashing waves, all four silhouetted against the bloodred sky. The shadow's mouth yawned wide as it looked back toward the beach where the four women danced, arms raised, bare feet following a complicated pattern in the sand, arms lifted toward the heavens.

The wind howled, rose to a shriek, and gusted toward the apparition, driving it so far away it was merely a spec on the horizon. Jonas stared at it, blinking. When he looked around, the glittering fireworks were gone and the wind had died down to nothing. He glanced at the beach below and saw Sarah,

Kate, Abigail, and Hannah lying unmoving on the sand.

"Get in the car, Damon." Jonas yanked the door open. "Hurry."

Damon did as directed, the echoes of the strange terror still gripping him. "What the hell is going on? I didn't see anything but fireworks, but I was . . ."

"Afraid," Jonas finished for him. "I don't know what the hell went on here tonight and I'm not sure if I want to know. Just get in the car. I need to take you home."

"Where's Sarah?"

"She's with her sisters on beach. I'll go down to them, but the things I have to say are better said alone." Grimly the sheriff slammed the door and drove faster than he should have to return Damon to the safety of his home. "Stay inside and use that security system Sarah's always fussing over. I'll call later to make certain everything's all right. My deputy, Jackson Deveau, will drive by several times tonight."

Jonas would have used the siren to return to the beach if it would have gotten him there faster. He was so angry he was certain he shouldn't go, he should stay away from the Drakes until his temper cooled and the fear left his body, but he couldn't just leave them lying exhausted on the beach.

He strode across the wet sand, fury building with every step he took. "What the hell did you all think you were doing?" The sight of their pale faces, worn with fatigue only stepped up his anger. "You were playing with something you sure as hell shouldn't have been playing with."

Sarah lifted a weak hand and waved him away. Hannah didn't look up and Kate and Abbey stared at him, their eyes enormous in their pale faces. He dropped onto his knees in the middle of them, reaching out to run his hand up and down over their arms to rub warmth back into them.

"What was it, Sarah?" he asked.

"Do you really want to know?"

She sounded so utterly weary he nearly kept his mouth shut. For once, Hannah wasn't sassing him and all of the Drakes looked frightened.

"Hell yes, I want to know."

"Death. You saw death, Jonas. It's how you're connected to us, why you are." Sarah glanced at her sisters and then back at his face. "You have a gift, just as we do. You deny yours and we embrace ours. Death showed you his face and he'll be back. We weakened him, but he'll be back and soon. He has too tight a grip on Damon." She said the last with a small hiccup in her voice.

At once her three sisters put their hands on her in an obvious attempt to comfort her. Jonas moved closer to Hannah and lifted her slightly so she could rest her head in his lap. He dragged Abigail closer as well until she had her head on his thigh. Sarah and Kate followed suit. He listened to the sound of the ocean, allowing the familiar melody to calm his mind and think more rationally.

"Why is death after Damon?" He felt like a fool asking the question. When the Drakes did their magic he preferred to be somewhere distant. He knew what they did and he even accepted it, but he always rationalized anything too spooky. Tonight didn't fit into a neat box and he sure as hell was never going to admit to seeing anything or having gifts or curses or anything else he couldn't find a scientific explanation for.

Sarah shrugged. "I don't think it much matters who death takes as long as he has someone. I don't want that someone to be Damon—or you."

"Me?"

"You stood in front of it. You confronted Death. Why did you do that?"

"Damn it, Sarah. It was a shadow. A shape on the wall and it looked as if it wanted to consume Wilder. I was afraid for him. I just did what seemed right."

"You brought yourself to his attention. You never want to do that," Sarah said. "Some things are better left alone."

"Well, you sure as hell must have his attention. And don't ever protect me like that again. I don't want any of you hurt trying to keep something like that off of me. I don't even know if I believe in all this mumbo jumbo. And if I don't, it can't hurt me." He wanted to shake some sense into them and at the same time he wanted to hold them close where he could protect them. Give him a flesh-and-blood criminal any day of the week, one he could see and fight. He forced calm into his voice when his heart was still pounding in fear for them. "Just don't ever do that again. I protect you. That's the way it's always been with us and that's the way it always will be. I'm taking you all up to the house and making you tea. Unless I decide to drop one or two of you in the ocean. I never want to talk about this again and if you bring it up, I swear I'm denying everything."

He wasn't making much sense but he didn't care. He just wanted them back inside their home where he knew they would be safe. And then he was going to think long and hard about getting drunk.

Chapter 8

⁓

"SO, SARAH," DAMON said, putting down his glass of iced tea as they sat on his porch. Damon and Sarah spent every minute they could find together. Taking walks on the beach. Working on a security system for his house. Lazy days of laughter and whispered confidences. Damon enjoyed every moment spent in her home, getting to know her sisters. He never ran out of things to say to Sarah and he loved her stories and open personality. There was sunshine in his life and its name was Sarah.

She took a handful of his chips and smiled at him. Overhead the seagulls circled, looking down with hopeful eyes. Damon had had no more unwelcome nighttime visitors and appreciated the regularity of the sheriff driving by to check the neighborhood.

Damon shook his head, dazzled by her smile. She could take every thought out of his head with that smile. "Sarah, are you afraid for me or for everyone else? It's occurred to me that there's always this buffer between everyone we run across and me. I didn't really notice at first, but last night I was thinking about it. I'm getting to know you and I think you prefer that your friends don't see you with me."

Sarah's breath caught in her throat at the hint of pain in his voice. The more time she spent with him, the more she wanted to be with him. And the dark shadow surrounding him gripped him all the harder. "I don't mind anyone seeing us together. You're the one worried about gossip. I'm used to it and it doesn't bother me."

"Then we'll go into town together." It was a challenge.

Sarah let out her breath. The early morning fog had burned off, leaving the sky an amazing shade of blue. She could see clouds gathering far out over the sea. She looked carefully at Damon, inspecting every inch of him. There was no dark shadow around him and his shoulders weren't hunched as if carrying a great weight. "Sounds great, if you're really certain you want to brave it."

He stood up and held out his hand to her. "Come on."

"Right now?" She hadn't expected he would really want to go, but she obediently took his hand and allowed him to help her up.

"Yes, while I have my courage up. Walking with you through town should set a match to the gossips. The story will spread like wildfire."

Sarah laughed softly, knowing it was true. Once they had walked the short distance to the town, she started in the direction of the grocery store, determined to get it over with.

"I feel a little sorry for Harrington," Damon said as he walked with Sarah along the main street of town. "He drops by the house sometimes and he's very nice." He reached out and tangled his fingers with Sarah's.

"Are you certain you want to do this?" Sarah's voice was skeptical. "Holding my hand in public is going to bring the spotlight shining very brightly on you. Rumors are going to race through town faster than a seagull flies. I know how much your privacy means to you."

"That was before I retired. When I worked from morning until night and had no life." Damon laughed softly. He was happy. Looking at her made him happy. Walking with her, talking with her. It was ridiculous how happy he was when he was in her company. It made no sense but he wasn't going to question a gift from the heavens. "We may as well give them something real to gossip about."

Sarah's laugh floated on the breeze, a melodious sound that

turned heads. "Not 'gossip,' Damon, it's 'news.' No one gossips here. You have to get it straight."

Damon listened to the sound of their shoes on the wooden walkway. Everything was so different with Sarah. He felt as if he'd finally come home. He looked around him to the picturesque homes, so quaint and unique. It no longer felt alien or hostile to him; the people were eccentric, but endearing. How had Sarah done that? Mysterious Sarah. Even the wind welcomed her back home. His fingers tightened around hers, holding her to him. He wasn't altogether certain Sarah was human and he feared she might fly away from him without warning, joining the birds out over the sea.

She waved to a young woman on a porch. "They're good people, Damon. You won't find more accepting people in your life than the ones living here."

"Even Harrington?" he teased.

"I feel a little sorry for him, too," Sarah answered seriously. "Most of the time, Jonas is a caring, compassionate man and very good with everyone, but he just refuses to see the truth about Hannah. He looks at her and only sees what's on the outside. She's always been beautiful. He was very popular with the girls in school, an incredible athlete, tons of scholarships, the resident dreamboat. He thought Hannah was stuck up because she never spoke to him. He made her life a living hell, teasing her unmercifully all through school. She's never forgiven him and he'll never understand why. He's a good man and he wasn't being malicious in school. From his perspective, he was just teasing. He has no idea Hannah is painfully shy and he never will."

Damon made a dissenting noise in his throat. "She's a supermodel, Sarah—on the cover of every magazine there is. She travels all over the world. And, I have to say, she appears very confident on every television and news interview and talk show I've seen her on. I would never associate her with the word 'shy.' "

"She hyperventilates before speaking in public; in fact, she carries a paper bag with her. Most of the talk show hosts and interviewers are careful with her. Because she's painfully shy doesn't mean she allows it to affect her life."

"Why wouldn't you just clue Harrington in?"

"Why should he judge Hannah so harshly, just because she

looks the way she does? My sister Joley is striking as well, although not in exactly the same way. Jonas would never dare torment her. All of my sisters are good-looking and he doesn't use that sarcastic tone on them. He only does it to Hannah and in front of everyone."

Damon heard the fierce protective note in her voice and smiled. He drew her closer beneath his broad shoulder. His Sarah. Without warning, fear struck, deep, haunting, sharp like a knife. His breath left his lungs. "Sarah? Are we thinking the same thing? I've never wanted someone in my life before. Not once. I've only just met you and can't imagine the rest of my life without you." He raked his fingers through his hair, his cane nearly hitting his head. "Do you know what I sound like? An obsessed stalker. I'm not like this with women, Sarah."

Her eyes danced. "That leaves wide-open territory, Damon. You're talking about a family with six sisters and a billion cousins. I have a million aunts and uncles. You can't leave yourself open like that or they're going to tease you unmercifully."

They halted in front of the grocery store. Damon faced her, catching her chin in his hand to tilt her face up to his. "I'm serious, Sarah. I know I want a future with you in it. I have to know we're on the same page."

Sarah went up on her toes to press a kiss to his mouth. "Here's a little news flash for you, Damon. I don't compromise my jobs by getting involved with my clients. I don't, as a rule, kiss strange men and spend the night wishing they'd make the big move."

"You want me to make a move on you?"

Sarah laughed, tugged at his hand, dragging him into the store. "Of course I do."

"Well, this is a hell of a time to tell me."

Inez was at the store window with three of her customers, staring at Sarah and Damon with their mouths open. Damon scowled at them. "Is it fly-catching season?"

Sarah squeezed his hand tightly in warning. All the while she was smiling serenely. "Inez! We just dropped in for a quick minute. Kate and Hannah and Abigail are in town for a few days and they can't wait to see you! Joley and Elle and Libby send their love and told me to tell you they hope to get back soon." Her voice was bright and cheerful, dispelling an air of gloom in the store. "You do know Damon, of course."

Inez nodded, her hawklike gaze narrowing in shock on their linked hands. Her throat worked convulsively. "Yes, of course I do. I didn't know you two were *intimate* friends."

Damon glared at her, daring the woman to imply anything else. Sarah simply laughed. "I snagged him the minute I saw him, Inez. You always told me to settle down with a good man and, well . . . here he is."

"I never guessed, and Mr. Wilder didn't say a single word," Inez said.

Damon forced a smile under the subtle pressure of Sarah's grip. Her nails were biting into his hand. "Call me Damon, Inez. I never managed to catch you alone." It was the best excuse he could come up with and sound plausible. It must have worked because Inez beamed at him, bestowing on him a smile she reserved for her closest friends. In spite of himself, Damon could feel a tiny glow of pleasure at the acceptance.

"How is everything lately?" Sarah asked before Damon could warn her it was a bad idea to get Inez started.

"Honestly, Sarah, Donna over at the gift shop is a lovely woman but she just doesn't understand the importance of re-cycling. Just this morning I saw her dump her papers right in with plastic. I've sorted for her many times and showed her the easiest way to go about it but she just can't get the hang of it. Be a dear and do something about it, won't you?"

Damon's mouth nearly fell open at the request. What did Inez want Sarah to do? Separate the woman's garbage for her?

"No problem, Inez. I'll go over there now. Damon and I are hoping some of our friends will help us with a small prob-lem. There are some strangers who have been in town, prob-ably for a week or two—three men. We'd like to know their whereabouts, their movements, that sort of thing. Unfortu-nately we don't have a clear description but one of them has a facial injury, most likely around his jaw. I'm hoping another might have gotten bitten by a tick." She paused, a wicked little grin playing around the corners of her mouth. "Maybe a lot of ticks."

"What have they done?" Inez asked, lowering her voice as if she'd joined a conspiracy.

"They tried to break into Damon's house. Jonas has all the information we could give him. He was going to check the hospital and clinic." She'd turned over the tranquilizer gun to him, too. "If someone spots them, or mentions them to you, would you mind giving me a call? And maybe it would be good to call Jonas, too."

"Now, dear, you know I don't believe in sticking my nose into anyone's business, but if you really need me to help you, I'll be more than happy to oblige," Inez said. "There are always so many tourists but we should be able to spot a man with something wrong with his jaw."

Sarah leaned over to kiss Inez affectionately. "You're such a good friend, Inez. I don't know what we'd all do without you." She turned to look at the three customers. "Irene, I hope you don't mind me bringing Damon when I call on you and Drew this afternoon." She wanted to assess Drew's condition before she brought her sisters over and raised Irene's hopes further. "We just want to visit with him a few minutes," she added hastily. "We won't tire him."

Irene's expression brightened considerably. "Thank you, Sarah; of course you can bring anyone you want with you. I told Drew you might be dropping by and he was so excited. He'll love the company. He rarely sees even his friends anymore."

"Good, I can't wait to see him again. Now don't go to any trouble, Irene. Last time I came to visit, you had an entire luncheon waiting." Sarah rubbed Damon's arm. "Irene is such a wonderful cook."

"Oh, she is," Inez agreed readily. "Her baked goods are always the first to go at every fundraiser."

Irene broke into a smile, looking pleased.

The warmth in Damon's heart rushed to his belly, heated his blood. Sarah spread sunshine. That had to be her secret. Wherever she went, she just spread goodwill to others because she genuinely cared about them. It wasn't that she was being merely tolerant; she liked her neighbors with all their idiosyncrasies. He couldn't help the strange feeling of pride sweeping through him. How had he gotten so lucky?

Damon pushed his sunglasses onto his nose as they meandered across the street. He saw they were heading toward the colorful gift shop. "Are you really going to sort some woman's garbage, Sarah?"

"Of course not, I'm just popping in to say hello. Maybe

our intruders will buy a memento of their stay or possibly a gift for someone. You never know, we may as well cover all the bases," Sarah replied blithely.

Damon laughed. "Sarah, honey, I hardly think kidnappers are going to take the time to buy a memento of their stay. I could be wrong, but it seems rather unlikely."

Sarah simply grinned at him. She took his breath away with her smile. She should have always been in his life. By his side. All those years working, never thinking about anything else, and Sarah had been somewhere in the world. If he had met her earlier, he might have retired sooner and . . .

"Do you have any idea how perfectly tempting your mouth is, Damon?" Sarah interrupted his thoughts, her voice matter-of-fact, intensely interested.

"Sarah! Sarah Drake! Yoo-hoo!" A tall woman of Amazonian proportions and extraordinary skin waved wildly, intercepting them. An older man, obviously her father, and a teenage boy followed her at a much more sedate pace.

The clouds, gathering ominously over the sea, so far away only minutes earlier, moved inward at a rapid rate. The wind howled, blowing in from the sea, carrying something dark and dangerous with it. Icy fingers touched Sarah's face, almost a caress of delight . . . or challenge. She watched Damon's face, his body, as he accepted the weight, a settling of his shoulders, small lines appearing near his mouth. He didn't appear to notice, already far too familiar with his grim companion.

She moved closer to Damon, a purely protective gesture as the two men approached them in the wake of the woman. The welcoming smile faded from Sarah's face. A shadow moved on the walkway, slithering along the ground, a wide dark net casting for prey. "Patsy, it's been a long time." But she was looking at the older man. "Mr. Granger. How nice to see you again. And Pete, I'm so glad we ran into you. I'm visiting Drew soon. I'll be able to tell him I saw you. I'll bet he'll be happy to hear from you."

Pete Granger scuffed the toe of his boot on the sidewalk. "I should go see him. It's been awhile. I didn't know what to say."

Sarah placed her hand on his shoulder. Damon could see she was worried. "You'll find the right thing to say to him. That's what friendship is, Pete, to be there in good and bad

times. The good is easy, the bad, well"—she shrugged—
"that's a bit more difficult. But you've always been incredibly
tough and Drew's best friend. I know you'll be there for him."

Pete nodded his head. "Tell him I'll be over this evening."

Sarah smiled her approval. "I think that's a great idea,
Pete." She touched the elder Granger with gentle fingers.
"How did your visit to the cardiologist go?"

"Why, Sarah," Patsy answered, "Dad doesn't have a cardiologist. There's nothing wrong with his heart."

"Really? It never hurts to be safe, Mr. Granger. Checkups
are always so annoying but ultimately necessary. Patsy, do you
remember that cardiologist my mother went to when we were
in our first year of college? In San Francisco?"

Patsy exchanged a long look with her father. "I do remember, Sarah. Maybe we could get him in next month when
things settle down at the shop."

"These things are always better if you insist on taking care
of them immediately," Sarah prompted. "This is Damon Wilder, a friend of mine. Have you three met yet?"

Damon was simply astonished. Pete was going to go visit
his very ill friend and Mr. Granger was going to see a cardiologist, all at Sarah's suggestion. He looked closer at the older
man. He couldn't see that Granger looked sick. What had
Sarah seen that he hadn't? There was no doubt in his mind
that the cardiologist was going to find something wrong with
Mr. Granger's heart.

Sarah asked the three of them to keep an eye out for strangers with bruises on their face or jaw and the trio agreed before
hurrying away.

"How do you do that?" Damon asked, intrigued. She was
doing something, knew things she shouldn't know.

"Do what?" Sarah asked. "I have no idea what you're talking about."

Damon studied her face there on the street with the sunlight
shining down on them. He couldn't stop looking at her,
couldn't stop wanting her. Couldn't believe she was real. "You
see something beyond the human eye, Sarah, something science can't explain. I believe in science, yet I can't find an
explanation for what you do."

Damon was looking at her with so much hunger, so much
stark desire in his expression, Sarah's heart melted on the spot

and her body went up in flames. "It's a Drake legacy. A gift." Wherever she had been going was gone out of her head. She couldn't think of anything but Damon and the need on his face, the hunger in his eyes. Her fingers tangled in the front of his shirt, right outside the gift shop in plain sight of the interested townspeople.

"The Drake gate prophecy forgot to mention the intensity of the physical attraction," she murmured.

A man could drown in her eyes, be lost forever. His hands tightened possessively, brought her closer to him, right up against his body. Every cell reacted instantly. Whips of lightning danced in his bloodstream while tongues of fire licked his skin, at the simple touch of her fully clothed body. What was going to happen when she was naked, completely bare beneath him? "I might not survive," he whispered.

"Would we care?" Sarah asked. She couldn't look away from him, couldn't stop staring into his eyes. She wanted him. Ached for him. Wanted to be alone with him. It didn't matter where, just that they were alone.

"You can't look at me like that," Damon said. "I'm going up in flames and I'm too damned old to be acting like a teenager."

"No, you're not," Sarah denied. "By all means, I don't mind at all." She half-turned toward the street, still in his arms. "I think Inez is falling out of her window. Poor thing, she's bound to lose her eyesight if she keeps this up. I should have suggested she get a new pair of glasses. I'll let Abigail suggest it. You have to be careful with Inez because she's so sensitive."

It was the way Sarah said it, so absolutely sincere, that tugged at his heartstrings. "I never could get along with people. Ever. Not even in college. Everyone always annoyed me. I preferred books and my lab to talking with a human being," he admitted, wanting her to understand the difference she'd made. He was actually beginning to care about Inez and that was plain damned scary. He was finding the townspeople interesting after seeing them through her eyes.

"Let's go back to my house," he suggested. "Didn't you say there could be bugs in that security system you installed?"

"I'm certain I need to check it over," Sarah agreed, "but I do have to make this one stop first. I promised Inez."

Chapter 9

THE SMALL GIFT shop was cheerful and bright. Celtic music played softly. New Age books and crystals of all colors occupied one side of the store while fairies and dragons and mythical creatures reigned supreme on the other. Damon had been prepared for clutter after the comments on the shop owner's lack of recycling education, but the store was spotless.

"I think Donna knows her recycling stuff," Damon whispered against Sarah's ear. "She probably brushed up after she saw Inez peering at her through the store window with her lips pursed and her hands on her hips." His teeth nibbled for just a moment, sending a tremor through her. "Let's get out of here while we have the chance."

Sarah shook her head. "I have an especially strong feeling we should talk with Donna today." She was frowning slightly, a puzzled expression on her face.

Damon felt something twist and settle around his heart. Knowledge blossomed. Belief. He was a man of logic and books, yet he knew Sarah was different. He knew she was magic. Mysterious Sarah was back home and with her, some undefined power that couldn't be ignored. He felt it now for himself, after having been in her presence. It was very real, something he couldn't explain but knew was there, deep inside of her.

His knowledge made it much easier to accept the amazing intensity of the chemistry between them. More than that, it helped him to believe in the powerful emotions already surfacing for her. How did one fall in love at first sight? He'd always scoffed at the idea, yet Sarah was wrapped securely around his heart and he had known her for only a few days.

"If you feel we should talk to Donna, then by all means, let's find the woman," he agreed readily. She had changed him for all time. *He* was different inside and he preferred the man he was becoming to the man he had been. If he spent too much time thinking about it, his feelings made no sense, but he didn't want to think about it. He simply accepted it, embraced the opportunity destiny had given him.

Sarah called out, moving through the store with the natural grace Damon had come to associate with her. "Donna's daughter went to school with Joley. Donna is a sweetheart, Damon—have you met her?" She peeked around the bead-curtained doorway leading to the back of the store.

"I've seen her," Damon said, "in Inez's store. She and Inez like to exchange sarcasm."

"They've been friends for years. When Inez was sick a few years ago, Donna moved into Inez's house and cared for her, ran her own gift shop and the grocery store. They just like to grouse at one another, but it's all in fun. The back screen is open. That's strange. Donna has a phobia about insects. She never leaves doors open." There was concern in her voice.

Damon followed Sarah through the beaded curtain, noting the neatly stacked paper tied with cord and the barrel of plastic labeled with inch-high letters. "I'd have to say Donna knows more about recycling than most people."

"Of course she does." Sarah's tone was vague, as if she wasn't paying much attention. "She just likes to give Inez something to say."

"You mean she does it on purpose?" Damon wanted to laugh but Sarah's behavior was making him uneasy. They stepped out of the shop onto a back porch.

The wind rushed them, coming at them from the sea. Coming from the direction of the cliff house. Sarah raised her face to the wind, closed her eyes for a moment. Damon watched her face, watched her body. There was a complete stillness about her. She was there with him physically, but he had the impression her spirit was riding on the wind. That mentally she was with her sisters in the cliff house.

The wind chilled him, raised goose bumps on his arms, sent a shiver of alarm down his back. Something was wrong. Sarah knew something was wrong and he knew it now as well.

Sarah opened her eyes and looked at him with apprehension. "Donna." She whispered the name.

The wind whipped leaves from the trees and whirled them in small eddies of chaos and confusion. Sarah watched the whirling mass of leaves intently. Her fingers closed around his wrist. "I don't think she's far but we have to hurry. Call the sheriff's office. Tell them to send an ambulance and to send a car over. I think one of your kidnappers did decide to shop at Donna's."

She started away from him, toward the small house that sat behind the gift shop. It was overgrown with masses of flowers and bushes, a virtual refuge in the middle of town. "Wait a minute!" Damon hesitated, torn between making the phone call and following Sarah. "What if someone's still there, and what if the sheriff thinks I'm a nut?"

"Someone is still there and just say I said hurry." Sarah flung the words back over her shoulder. She was moving fast, yet silently, lithely, so graceful she reminded him of a stalking animal.

Damon swore under his breath and hurried back inside the store. Inez was standing just inside the beaded curtain. Her face was very pale. "What is it?" she demanded, her hand fluttering to her heart.

"Sarah said to call the sheriff and tell them to hurry. She also said to call an ambulance. Would you do that so I can make certain nothing happens to Sarah?" Damon spoke gently, afraid the older woman might collapse.

Inez lifted her chin. "You go, I'll have a dozen cops here immediately."

Damon breathed a sigh of relief and hurried after Sarah. She was already out of his sight, lost behind the rioting explosion of flowers. He silently cursed his bum leg. He could go anywhere if he went slowly enough but he couldn't run and even walking fast was dangerous. His leg would simply give out.

His heart was pounding so hard in his chest he feared it would explode. Sarah in danger was terrifying. He had thought there was nothing left for him, yet she had come into his life at his darkest hour and brought hope and light. Laughter and compassion. She was even teaching him to appreciate Inez. Damon swore again, pressing his luck, using his cane to hold back the bushes while he tried to rush over the cobblestones Donna had so painstakingly used to build the pathway between her house and her shop.

A soft hiss to his left gave Sarah's position away. She was inching her way toward the door of Donna's house, using several large rhododendrons as cover. Her hand signal was clear: she wanted him to crouch low and stay where he was. A humiliating thought. Sarah racing to the rescue while he hid in the bushes. The worst of it was, he could see that she was a professional. She moved like one, and she had produced a gun from somewhere. It fit into her hand as if she were so familiar with it, the gun was a part of her.

Damon realized, for all their long talks together, he didn't know Sarah very well at all. His heart and mind and soul wanted and needed her, but he didn't know her. Enthralled, he watched as she gained the porch. Even the wind seemed to have stilled, holding its breath.

Sarah turned back to look up at the sky, to lift her arms toward the clouds. Her face was toward the cliff house. Damon had a sudden vision of her sisters standing on the battlements in front of the rolling sea, raising their arms in unison with Sarah. Calling on the wind, calling on the elements to bind their wills together.

The wind moaned softly, carrying the sound of a melodious song, so faint he couldn't catch the words but he knew the voices were female. Dark threads spun into thick clouds overhead and the wind rushed at the house, rattling the windows and shaking the doors. The sky darkened ominously, fat drops of rain splattered the roof and yard. Damon tasted salt in the air. The rain seemed to come from the ocean itself, as if the wind, in answer to some power, had driven the salt water from the sea and spread it over the land.

The wind pulled back, reminiscent of a wave, then rushed

again, this time with a roar of rage, aiming at the entry. Under the assault, the door burst inward, allowing the chilling wind into the house. Sarah rolled in behind it, as papers and magazines flew in all directions, providing a small distraction. She was already up on one knee in a smooth motion, tracking with her gun.

"I don't want to have to shoot you, but I will," she said. The words carried clearly to Damon although her voice was very low. "Put the gun down and kick it away from you." Damon hurried up the porch steps. He could see that Sarah's hand was rock steady. "Donna, don't try to move, an ambulance is on the way." Her gaze hadn't shifted from the man standing over Donna's body.

Damon could see the lump on Donna's head, the blood spilling onto the thick carpet. His fingers tightened around his cane until his knuckles turned white. He transferred his hold to a two-handed grip. Fury shook him at the sight of the woman on the floor and the man he recognized standing over her.

"Damon." Sarah's voice was gentle but commanding. "Don't."

He hadn't realized he had taken an aggressive step forward. Sarah hadn't turned her head, hadn't taken her alert gaze from Donna's attacker, but she somehow knew his intention. He forced himself back under control.

"Why would you attack a helpless woman?" Damon asked. He was shaking with anger, with the need to retaliate.

"Don't engage with him," Sarah counseled. "I hear a siren. Will you please see if it's the sheriff?"

Damon turned and nearly ran over Inez. He caught her as she tried to rush to Donna's side. "You can't get between Sarah and the man who attacked Donna," he said. Inez felt light and fragile in his hands. She never seemed old, yet now he could see age lined her face. She looked so anxious he was afraid for her. Very gently he drew her away from the entrance, pulling her to one side.

The wind whipped through the room, sent loose papers once more into the air. Inez shivered and reached to close the door on the chilling sea breeze.

"No!" Sarah's voice was sharp this time, unlike her.

It was enough to stimulate Damon into action. He held the

door open to the elements. It was only then that he felt the subtle flow of power entering with the wind. Faintly he could hear, or imagined that he heard, the chanting carried from the direction of the ocean . . . or the cliff house.

He studied Donna's assailant, one of the men who had tortured him. The man who had pressed a gun to Dan's head and pulled the trigger. Why was he simply standing there motionless? Was it really the threat of Sarah's gun?

Damon had no doubt that she would shoot, but would that be enough to intimidate a man like this one? He doubted it. There was something else in the room, something holding the killer.

A sense of rightness stole into his heart, carried with it a sense of peace. Sarah was a woman of silk and steel. She was magnificent.

"Jonas is coming," Inez whispered to Damon. "Sarah's going to have a problem. She'll be weak and sick after this. She won't want anyone to see her like that."

Damon could see the acceptance of his relationship with Sarah in Inez's expression. It made him feel as if he truly belonged. Inez's approval meant more to him than it should have, made him feel a part of the close-knit community instead of the outsider he always seemed to be wherever he went.

He nodded his head, pretending to understand, determined to be there for Sarah the way she seemed to be for everyone else.

Jonas Harrington came through the door first, his eyes hard and unflinching. He had Donna's assailant in handcuffs immediately. Sarah sank back on her haunches, her head bowed. She wiped sweat from her brow with the back of a trembling hand. Damon went to her immediately, helping her up, forcing her to lean on him when she didn't want to, when she was worried about his hip and leg.

Sarah went down the hall with Damon's help, found a chair in the kitchen where she could sit. She looked up at him and smiled her appreciation. That was all. And it was everything. He got her a glass of water, helped her steady her hands enough to drink it. She recovered fairly quickly, but she remained pale.

"Are your sisters feeling the same effects?" he asked.

Sarah nodded. "It isn't the same as casting. It takes a tremendous amount of our energy to hold someone against his or her will. It wasn't in his nature to be passive." She held out her hand. "I'm doing better. I need to eat something and sleep for a little while." She sighed. "I promised Irene I'd go visit Drew tonight but I don't have any strength left after this, not the kind I'd need to help them." She pressed her fingertips to her temples. "I can't really do anything for Drew and Irene knows that. Extending his life might not be the best thing. If only Libby were here."

"Sarah." He spoke in his most gentle tone. "Leave it alone for now. Let me take you home; I'll fix you a good meal and you can sleep. I'll talk to Irene myself. She'll understand."

"How did you know my sisters were helping me?"

"I felt them," he replied. "Are you steady enough to talk with the sheriff?"

She nodded. "And I want to make certain Donna's all right."

When they returned to the living room, Harrington already had Donna's assailant in the squad car. Donna burst into tears, clinging to Sarah and Inez, making Damon feel helpless and useless but filled with a deep sense of pride in Sarah and her sisters.

"Why did he attack you, Donna?" Sarah asked.

"I noticed he had your earring, Sarah. The one Joley made for you. He was wearing it. It's one of a kind and I thought you must have lost it. So I asked him about it. He hit me hard and dragged me out of the store back into my house. He kept asking me questions about you and about Mr. Wilder."

Sarah pressed her hand against Donna's wound, just for a moment. Damon watched her face carefully, watched her skin grow paler until she swayed slightly with weariness. Sarah leaned down and kissed Donna's cheek. "You'll be fine. Don't worry about the store, we'll lock up for you."

"I'm going to the hospital with her," Inez said, glaring at the paramedics as if daring them to deny her. She held Donna's hand as they took her out.

"Sarah?" Jonas Harrington stood waiting against the wall. "You have a permit to carry that gun?"

"You know I do, Jonas," she replied. "You've seen it more than once. Yes, it's up-to-date. And I didn't shoot the man, although I was inclined to with Donna lying on the floor bleeding. And he is wearing my earring. I want it back."

"I'll get it back for you," Jonas was patient. "I know you're tired, but I need you to answer a few questions."

"That's one of the men who kidnapped me. He's the one who killed my assistant," Damon explained. "The other two must be staying somewhere in town. It shouldn't be that hard to find them now that we have him."

"I'll find them." Jonas's voice was grim. "Sarah, will you come by the office later and give me a full statement? I've sent the perp in the squad car down to the office. There's already an outstanding warrant for his arrest and the feds are going to be swarming all over this place as soon as we notify them. They're going to want to talk to the two of you, so you'd better go rest while you can."

Damon circled Sarah's shoulders with his arm. "Can you give us a ride to my place, Sheriff?"

"Sure. Let's lock up and get out of here before Sarah keels over and her sisters haul us both over the coals. You've never seen them en masse, coming after you." He shuddered. "It's a scary sight, Wilder."

"You're the only one it's ever happened to so far," Sarah pointed out.

Chapter 10

⁓

•

DAMON STARED DOWN into Sarah's sleeping face. She was beautiful lying there in the middle of his bed. He had been standing there, leaning against the wall, for some time just watching over her. Guarding her. It seemed rather silly and melodramatic when she was the one with the gun and the training, but it felt as necessary to him as breathing.

Where had such a wealth of feeling come from nearly over-night? Could a man fall deeply in love with a woman so quickly? She was everything and more than he'd ever thought of or dreamed about. How could anyone not love Sarah with her compassion and tolerance and understanding? She genu-inely cared about the people in her town. Somehow that deep emotion was rubbing off on him.

She could have been killed. The thought hit him hard. A physical blow in the pit of his stomach. How was it possible to feel so much for one person when he'd just met her? His entire life he'd barely noticed people, let alone cared about their lives. From the moment he'd heard her name whispered on the wind, he knew, deep down where it counted, that she would change his life for all time.

Their walks together, all the times on the beach, whispering in his house, or hers, even spending time with her family had only strengthened his feelings for her.

Sarah opened her eyes and the first thing she saw was Damon's face. He was leaning against the far wall, simply watching her. She could see his expression clearly, naked desire, mixed with knowledge of their future. His emotions were stark and raw and so real it brought tears to her eyes. Damon hadn't expected to like her, let alone feel anything else for her.

She held out her hand to him. "Don't stand over there all alone. You aren't alone anymore and neither am I."

He heard the invitation in her voice and his body began to stir in anticipation. But he stood there drinking her in. Wanting her in so many ways that weren't just physical.

"You weren't, you know, Sarah. You've never been alone. You don't need me in the same way I need you. You have a family and they wrap you up in love and warmth and support. I never considered the value of family and love. Sharing a day with someone you care about is worth all the gold in the world. I didn't know that before I met you."

She sat up, studying him with her cool gaze. Assessing. Liking what she saw. Damon didn't know why but he could see it on her face. "I'm glad then, Damon, if I gave you such a gift. My family is my treasure."

He nodded. What would it be like to wake up every morning and hear her voice? There was always a caress in her voice, a stroking quality that he felt on his skin. Deep in his body. "And you're my treasure, Sarah. I had no idea I was even capable of feeling this way about anyone."

Sarah smiled. The smile she seemed to reserve for him. It lit up her face and made her eyes shine, but more, it lit up his insides so that he burned with something indefinable. "You brought me life, Sarah. You handed me my life. I existed before I met you, but I wasn't living."

"Yes, you were, Damon. You're a brilliant man. The things you created made our world safer. I watch your face light up when you tell me about other ideas you have and what the possibilities are. That's living."

"I had nothing else but my ideas." He straightened suddenly, coming away from the wall, walking toward her, confidence on his face. "That was how I escaped, into my brain and the endless ideas I could find there." He traced the classic lines of her face, her cheekbones. Her generous mouth. "Take off your blouse, Sarah. I want to see you."

A faint blush stole into her cheeks but her hands went to the tiny pearl buttons on her blouse and slowly began to slide the edges apart. His breath caught in his throat as he watched her. Sarah didn't try to be sexy, there was never anything affected about her, yet it was the sexiest thing he'd ever seen. The edges of her blouse slowly gaped open, to reveal her lush creamy flesh beneath it. She had a woman's body, shaped to please a man with soft curves and lines.

Her breasts were covered with fine white lace. Sarah stood up, her body very close to his. Damon felt a rush of heat take him, a whip of lightning dance through his body. His blood thickened and pooled. His body hardened almost to the point of pain. He embraced it, reveled in the intensity of his need for her.

"You're so beautiful, Sarah. Inside and out. I still can't believe I could go from living in hell straight to paradise."

She reached for him. "I'm not like that at all, Damon. I'm not truly beautiful, not by any stretch of the imagination. I'm not even close. And living with me would not be paradise. I'm outspoken and like my way."

With exquisite tenderness, he bent his head to find her mouth with his. For a moment they were lost together, transported out of time by the magic flowing between them. When Damon lifted his head to look down at her, his gaze was hungry. Needy. Possessive. "You're beautiful to me, Sarah. I will never see you any other way. And lucky for you, I'm stubborn and very outspoken myself. I think those are admirable traits."

"That is lucky," she murmured, allowing her eyelashes to drift down and her head to fall back as he pulled her closer, his mouth breathing warm, moist air over her nipple right through the white lace. Her arms cradled his head as she arched her body, offering temptation, offering heaven.

His mouth was hot and damp as it closed over her breast. Fire raced through her, through him. Sarah gave herself up to sensual pleasure as his tongue danced and teased and his mouth suckled strongly right through the lace. He took his time, a lazy, leisurely exploration, his hands shaping her body, using the pads of his fingers as a blind man would to trace every curve and hollow. Memorizing her. Worshipping her.

Sarah was lost in sensation. Drowning in it. She couldn't remember him unsnapping her jeans, or even unzipping them. But her lacy bra had long ago floated to the floor and somehow he managed to push denim from her hips. In a haze of need and heat she stepped out of the last of her clothes.

He was never hurried, even as his mouth fused once more with hers and she was trying to drag his shirt from his broad shoulders so she could be skin to skin with him. He was patient and thorough, determined to know her body, to find every hidden trigger point that had her gasping in need. His hands moved over her, finding the shadows and hollows, tracing her ribs lovingly. He allowed Sarah to drag his clothes from his body, not appearing to notice or care, so completely ensnared by the wonders of giving her pleasure. He loved the little gasps and soft cries that came from deep in her throat.

Sarah. So responsive and giving. He should have known she would be a generous lover, merging with him so completely, giving of herself endlessly. Her selfless gift only made him want to be equally generous. For the first time his scars weren't shameful and something he hid. When her fingertips traced them, there was no reluctance, no shrinking away from the ugly memories of torture and murder. She soothed his body, caressing his skin, arousing him further, eager to touch him, wanting him with the same urgency he wanted her.

He lowered her slowly to the sheets, following her down, settling his body over hers. Her face was beautiful as she stared up at him. He kissed her eyes, the tip of her nose, the corners of her mouth.

Everywhere he touched her he left flames behind. Sarah was astonished at the sheer intensity of the fire. He was so unhurried, taking his time, but she was going up in flames, burning inside and out, needing his body in hers. She heard her own voice, a soft plea for mercy as his lips nipped over her navel, went lower. His hands moved with assurance, finding the insides of her thighs, the damp heat waiting for him at the junction of her legs.

"Damon." She could barely breathe his name. Her breath seemed to have permanently left her body. There wasn't enough air in the room.

His finger pushed deep inside her, a stroke of sensuality that drove her out of her mind. Every sane thought she'd ever had was gone. There was a roaring in her head when his mouth found her, claimed her, branded her his. She couldn't keep her hips still, writhing until his arms pinned her there, while his hot mouth ravaged her and wave after wave of pleasure rippled through her body with the force of the booming ocean. Her fingers tangled in his hair, her only anchor to hold her to earth while she soared free, gasping out his name.

Damon moved then, blanketing her completely, his hips settling into the cradle of hers. He was thick and hard and throbbing with his own need. He pushed deep inside of her, his voice hoarse as he cried out as the sweeping pleasure engulfed him. She was hot and slick and tight, a velvet fist closing around him, gripping with a fire he'd never known. Sarah. Magical Sarah.

He began to move. Never hurried. Why would he hurry his first time with Sarah? He wanted the moment to last forever. To be forever for both of them. He loved watching her face as he moved with her. As his body surged deep and her body took him in, her secret sanctuary of heat and joy. Her hips rose to join him, matching his rhythm, tilting to take him deeper and deeper with every stroke, wanting every inch of him. Wanting his possession as much as he wanted her.

The fire just kept building. He was in complete control one moment, certain of it, reveling in it, and then the pleasure was almost too much to bear, hitting him with the force of a freight train, starting in his toes and blowing out the top of his head. His voice was lifted with hers, merged and in perfect unison.

He could feel the aftershocks shaking her, tightening around him, drawing them ever closer. They lay together, not daring to move, unable to move, their hearts wild and lungs starving for air, their arms wrapped tightly around one another. The ocean breeze was gentle on the window, whispering soothing sounds while the sea sang to them with rolling waves.

Damon found peace. She lay in his arms, occasionally rousing herself enough to kiss his chest, her tongue tracing a scar. Each time she did so, his body tightened in answer and hers responded with another aftershock. They were merged so completely, so tightly bound together he couldn't tell where he started or left off.

"Stay with me the rest of the day, Sarah. All night. We can do anything you like. Just be with me." He propped himself up on his elbows to take most of his weight off of her. He wanted to be locked together, one body, sharing the same skin, absorbing her.

She reached up to trace the lines of his face. "I can't think of anywhere I'd rather be or who I'd rather be spending time with."

"Do you wonder why you chose me? I stopped asking myself that question and just accept it. I'm grateful, Sarah."

"I look at you and I just know. Who can say why one heart belongs to another? I don't ask myself that question either, Damon. I'm just grateful the gate opened for you." She laughed with sudden amusement. "It has occurred to me you might be seducing me to try to get the secret of paint preservation."

He tangled his fingers with hers, stretched her arms above her head. "It did seem a good idea. Maybe one of these days I'll be able to speak when I'm making love to you and I'll be able to pry the secret out of you."

"Good plan; it might work, too, if I could manage to speak when you're making love to me." She gasped as he lowered his head to her breast. "Damon." Her body was hypersensitive, but she arched into the heat of his mouth.

"I'm sorry, you looked so tempting, I couldn't help myself. How do you feel about just lying here without a stitch on while I build a fire and cook something for you to eat? I'm not certain I can bear for you to put your clothes back on." His teeth scraped back and forth over her breast. His tongue laved her nipple.

Sarah's entire body tightened, every muscle going taut. "You just want me to be lying here waiting for you?"

"Waiting *eagerly* for me," he corrected. "Needing me would be good. I wouldn't mind if you just lay here on my bed thinking of my body buried inside you."

"I see. I thought it might be better if I just followed you around, looking at you, touching you while you worked. Inspiring you. I have my ways, you know, of inspiring you."

There was a wicked note in her voice that made his entire body aware of how receptive and pliant she was. He was all at once as hard as a rock, thick with need. Damon watched her eyes widen in pleased surprise. Desire spread through both of them, sheer bliss. "I've never felt this way with any other woman, Sarah. I know it isn't possible. I think you really could walk on water."

"For a man who spent a lot of time in a laboratory, you know your way around women," she pointed out. He was moving with that exquisite slowness he used to drive her straight up the wall. The friction on her already sensitive body was turning her inside out. It didn't matter how many times she went over the edge, Damon moved with almost perfect insight, perfect knowledge of what she needed. What she wanted.

"I can read your face and your body," he said. "I love that, Sarah. You don't hold anything back from me."

"Why should I?" Why would she want to when the rewards were so great? If Damon was the man destiny insisted would be the love of her life, her best friend and partner, she was willing to accept whatever he had to give.

Sarah loved the sound of his voice, the thoughtful intelligent way he approached every subject. And she loved his complete honesty. There was that same raw honesty in his lovemaking. He gave himself to her, even as he took her for his own. She *felt* his possession deep in her soul, branded into her very bones.

There was that patient thoroughness and then, when he was fully aroused, his body was a driving force, each stroke hard and fast and insistent, taking them both soaring out over the sea, free-falling through time and space until neither could move again.

Damon held her in his arms, curled next to her, not wanting to end the closeness between them. They were completely sated for the moment, exhausted, breathing with effort, yet there was the same sense of absolute peace. "Sarah." He whispered her name, a tribute more than anything else.

"All those things you feel about me," she said, snuggling closer to him, "I feel about you. I didn't want anyone in my life any more than you did. I sometimes tire of giving pieces of myself to other people, yet I can't help myself. I find places I'm safe, places where I'm alone and can crawl into a hole and disappear for a while."

"Now you have me. I'll be your sanctuary, Sarah. I don't mind running interference in the times you need to regroup." His smile was against her temple. "I've never had a problem bossing people. I've always had a difficult time communicating with people. They never understood what I was talking about and it drove me crazy. Sometimes when you have an idea and it's so clear and you know it's right, you just have to share it with someone. But no one has ever been there."

Sarah kissed his fingertips. "You can tell me any idea that comes into your head, Damon. I admire you." Her smile was in her voice. "And I'm *very* good at communicating so you'll never have to worry about that."

"I noticed," he said. "Speaking of communication, I made certain the curtains couldn't creep open. I safety-pinned them together just in case any of your sisters decided to go up on the battlements to look through the telescope."

Sarah laughed just as he knew she would. "They know I'm with you. They wouldn't invade our privacy when we're really making love. They simply love to tease me. You'll have a lot of that come morning."

Damon didn't mind at all. He tightened his arms around her and found he was looking forward to anything her sisters might want to dish out.

Chapter 11

~

"OKAY, HAVE ANY of you really read this prophecy?" Kate demanded as they walked along the sidewalk toward Irene's house. The fog was thick and heavy, lying over the sea and most of the town like a blanket. "Because I have and it isn't good news for the rest of us."

"I don't like the sound of that," Hannah said. "Maybe we shouldn't ask. Can ignorance keep us safe?"

"What prophecy?" Damon asked curiously. They had spent the morning together over breakfast, teasing him unmercifully, making Sarah blush and hide her face against his chest. He had felt just as he anticipated—part of a family—and the feeling was priceless.

Sarah laughed in wicked delight. "You all thought it was so funny when it was happening to me, but *I* had read the entire thing. I know what's in store for the rest of you. One by one you'll fall like dominoes."

Abbey made a face at Sarah. "Not all of us, Sarah. I don't believe in fate."

The other girls roared with laughter. Sarah slipped her hand into Damon's. "The prophecy is this horrible curse put on the seven sisters. Well, we thought it was a curse. I'm not so certain now that I've met you."

His eyebrow shot up. "Now I'm really curious. I'm involved with this prophecy in some way?"

The four women laughed again. The sound turned heads up and down the street. "You are the prophecy, Damon," Kate said. "The gate opened for you."

Sarah gave a short synopsis of the quote. "Seven sisters intertwined, controlling elements of land, sea, and air, cannot control the fate they flee. One by one, oldest to last, destiny will find them. When the locked gate swings open in welcome, the first shall find true love. There's a lot more, but basically it goes on to say, one by one all the other sisters shall be wed."

Sarah's three sisters muttered and grumbled and shook their heads. Damon burst out laughing. "You have to marry me, don't you? I've been wondering how I was going to manage to keep you, but you don't have a choice. I like that prophecy. Does it say anything about waiting on me hand and foot?"

"Absolutely not," Sarah replied and glared at her laughing sisters. "Keep it up—the rest of you, even you, Abbey, are going to see me laughing at you." She tightened her fingers around Damon's hand. "We all made a pact when we were kids to keep the gate padlocked and never really date so we could be independent and free. We've always liked our life together . . . and poor Elle—the thought of seven daughters is rather daunting."

"Thank heavens Elle gets all the kids," Abbey said. "I am going to have one, and only because if I don't the rest of you will drive me crazy."

"Why does Elle have to have the seven daughters?" Damon asked.

"The seventh daughter always has seven daughters," Kate explained. "It's been that way for generations. I've been reading the history of the Drake family and I've found over the years, from all the entries made, we at least have a legacy of happy marriages." She smiled at Damon. "So far I haven't seen anything that indicated waiting on the man hand and foot but I'll keep looking."

"While you're at it, will you also keep an eye out for the traditional obey-the-husband rule?" Damon asked. "I've always thought that word was crucial in the marriage ceremony. Without it, a man doesn't stand a chance."

"Dream on," Sarah said. "That will never happen. The problem with being locked up in a stuffy lab all of your life is becoming evident. Delusions start early."

They were passing a small, neat home with a large front yard surrounded by the proverbial white picket fence. An older couple was working on a fountain in the middle of a bed of flowers. Sarah suddenly stopped, turned back to look at the house and the couple. A shadow slithered across the roof. A hint of something seen, then lost in the fog. "I'll just be a minute." She waved to the older couple and both stood up immediately and came over to the fence.

Sarah's sisters looked at one another uneasily. Damon followed Sarah. "It isn't necessary to speak to every citizen in town," he advised Sarah's back. She ignored his good judgment and struck up a conversation with the older couple anyway. Damon sighed. He had a feeling he was going to be following Sarah and talking to everyone they met for the rest of his life.

"Why, Sarah, I'd heard you were back. Is everything all right? I haven't seen you for what is it now? Two years?" The older woman spoke as she waved to the sisters.

"Mrs. Darden, I was admiring your yard. Did you remodel your house recently?"

The Dardens looked at one another then back to Sarah. Mr. Darden cleared his throat. "Yes, Sarah, the living room and kitchen. We came into a little money and we always wanted to fix up the house. It's exactly the way we want it now."

"That's wonderful." She rubbed the back of her neck and looked up at the roof. "I see you've got ladders out. Are you re-roofing?"

"It was leaking this winter, Sarah," Mr. Darden said. "We lost a tree some months ago and a branch hit the house. We've had trouble ever since."

"It looks as if you're doing the work yourself," Sarah observed and rubbed the back of her neck a second time.

Damon reached out to massage her neck with gentle fingers. The tremendous tension he felt in her neck and shoulders kept him silent. Wondering.

"I hear Lance does wonderful roofing, Mr. Darden. He's

fast and guarantees his work. Rather than you climbing around on the roof, wasting your time when you could be gardening." She turned her head slightly to look at Damon. "Mr. Darden is renowned for his garden and flowers. He wins every year at the fair for his hybrids."

Damon could see shadows in her eyes. He smiled at her, leaned forward to brush a gentle kiss on the top of her head when she turned back to the Dardens. "Lance probably needs the work and you'd be doing him such a favor."

Mrs. Darden tugged at her husband's hand. "Thank you, Sarah, it's good advice and we'll do that. I've been worrying about Clyde up there on that roof but . . ." She trailed off.

"I think you're right, Sarah," Mr. Darden suddenly agreed. "I think I'll call Lance straightaway."

Sarah shrugged with studied casualness but Damon felt her shoulders sag in relief. "I can't wait for the fair this year to see your beautiful entries. I really wanted you to meet Damon Wilder, a friend of mine. He bought the old Hanover place." She smiled sweetly at Damon to include him. "I know you're often in the garden and working on your lovely yard—have you noticed any strangers around that were asking questions or making you feel uncomfortable?"

The Dardens looked at one another. "No, Sarah, I can't say that we have," Mrs. Darden answered, "but then we strictly mind our own business. You know I've always believed in staying out of my neighbors' affairs."

"It's just that with you working outdoors so much I thought you might be able to keep an eye out for me and give me a call if anything should look suspicious," Sarah said.

"You can count on us, Sarah," Mr. Darden said. "I just bought myself a new pair of binoculars and sitting on my front porch I have a good view of the entire street!"

"Thank you, Mr. Darden," Sarah said. "That would be wonderful. We're just on our way to visit Irene and Drew."

The smile faded from Mrs. Darden's face. "Oh, that's so sad, Sarah, I hope you can help them. When is Libby going to come home? She would be such a help. How's she doing these days?"

"Libby's overseas right now, Mrs. Darden," Sarah said. "She's doing fine. Hopefully she'll be able to get home soon. I'll tell her you were inquiring about her."

"I heard the awful news on Donna," Mrs. Darden continued. "Are these strangers involved in her attack? I heard you shot one of them. I don't believe in violence as a rule, Sarah, now, you know that, but I hope you did enough damage that he'll think twice before he attacks another woman."

"Donna's going to be fine," Sarah assured her, "and I didn't shoot him."

Mrs. Darden patted Sarah's shoulder. "It's all right dear, I understand."

Sarah turned away with a cheery wave. The sisters erupted into wild laughter. Damon shook his head incredulously. "She thinks you shot that man. Even now, with you denying it, she thinks you shot him."

"True." Sarah pinned him with a steely gaze. "She also believes someone saw me walk on water. Now who could have started that rumor?"

Hannah tugged at Damon's sleeve in a teasing way, a gesture of affection for her. "That was a good one, Damon, I wish I'd thought of it."

Kate threw back her head and laughed, her wild mane of hair blowing around her in the light breeze. "That was priceless. And you should hear what they're saying about you. The whisper is, you're some famous wizard Sarah's been studying under."

"Now really," Sarah objected, "at least they could have said *he's* been studying under *me*. I swear chauvinism is still rearing its ugly head in this century."

Damon could feel a glow spreading. He felt a part of their family. He belonged with them, in the midst of their laughter and camaraderie. He didn't feel on the outside looking in, as he had most of his life. Sarah's sisters seemed to accept him readily into their lives and even their hearts. Tolerance and acceptance seemed a big part of Sarah's family. It suddenly occurred to him, even with a threat hanging over his head, that he'd spent less time thinking of past trauma and more about the present and future than he had in months.

"I think I like being thought of as a wizard," Damon mused.

"Sarah says you're a brain." Kate waved at Jonas Harrington as he cruised by them in his patrol car.

"What are you doing?" Hannah hissed, smacking Kate's

hand down. "Don't be nice to that idiot. We should make him drive into a ditch or something."

"Don't you dare," Sarah told her sister sternly. "I mean it, Hannah, you can't use our gifts for revenge. Only for good. Especially now."

"It would be for good," Hannah pointed out. "It would teach that horrible man some manners. Don't look at him. And Damon, stop smiling at him. We don't want him stopping to talk." She made a growling noise of disgust in the back of her throat as the patrol car pulled to the sidewalk ahead of them. "Now see what you've done?" She threw her hands into the air as Harrington got out of his car. A sudden rush of wind took his hat from his head and sent it skittering along the gutter.

"Very funny, Baby Doll," Harrington said. "You just have to show off, don't you? I guess that pretty face of yours just doesn't get you enough attention."

Kate and Sarah both put a restraining hand on Hannah's arm. Sarah stepped slightly between the sheriff and her sister. "Did you get anything out of your prisoner, Jonas?" Her voice was carefully pleasant.

Jonas continued to pin Hannah with his ice cold gaze. "Not much, Sarah, and we still haven't located the other two men you say were at Wilder's house the other night. You might have called me instead of charging in on your own."

Hannah stirred as if she might protest. Damon could see the fine tremor that ran through her body but her sisters edged protectively closer to Hannah and she stilled.

"Yes, next time, Jonas, I'll do that: leave the three men with guns trained on the window, sneaking up on the house, while I go find a phone and call you. Darn, those cell phones just don't seem to work on the coast most of the time, do they?" Sarah smiled right through her sarcasm. "Next time I'll drive out to the bluff and give you a call before I charge in on my own."

Jonas's gaze didn't leave Hannah's face. "You do that, Sarah." He knotted his fists on his hips. "Did any of you consider Sarah might have been killed? Or how I might feel if I found her dead body? Or if I had to go up to your house and tell you she was dead? Because I thought a lot about that last night."

"I thought about it," Damon said. "At least about Sarah being killed on my account." He reached out to settle his fingers possessively around the nape of her neck. "It scared the hell out of me."

Kate and Abbey exchanged looks with Hannah. "I didn't think of that," Kate admitted. "Not once."

"Thanks a lot, Jonas," Sarah said. "Now they're all going to be making me crazy, wanting me to change my profession. I'm a security expert."

"It may beat being a Barbie doll, but I think you went overboard, Sarah," Jonas replied. "A librarian sounds nice to me."

Hannah clenched her teeth but remained silent. The wind rushed through the street, sweeping the sheriff's hat toward a storm drain. It landed in a dark puddle of water and disappeared from sight.

Harrington swore under his breath and stalked back to his car, his shoulders stiff with outrage.

"Hannah," Kate scolded gently, "that wasn't nice."

"I didn't do it," Hannah protested. "*I* would have had the oak tree come down and drive him underground feet first."

Abbey and Kate looked at Sarah. She merely raised her eyebrow. "I believe Irene and Drew are waiting."

Damon burst out laughing. "I can see I'm going to have to watch you all the time." Why did it seem perfectly normal that the Drake sisters could command the wind? Even Harrington treated it as a normal phenomenon.

They stopped in front of Irene's house. Damon could see all the women squaring their shoulders as if going into battle. "Sarah, what do you think you can do for Drew? Surely you can't cure what's wrong with him."

Sadness crept into her eyes. "No, I wish I had that gift. Libby is the only one with a real gift for healing. I've seen her work miracles. But it drains her and we don't like her doing it. There's always a cost, Damon, when you use a gift."

"So you aren't conjuring up spells with toads and dragon livers?" He was half-serious. He could easily picture them on broomsticks, flying across the night sky.

"Well . . ." Abbey drew the word out, looking mischievously from one sister to the other. "We can and do if the situation calls for it. Drakes have been leaving each other recipes and spells for hundreds of years. We prefer to use the power within us, but conjuring is within the rules."

"You never let me," Hannah groused.

"No, and we're not going to either," Sarah said firmly. "Actually, Damon, to answer your question, we hope to assess the situation and maybe buy Drew a little more time. If the quality of his life is really bad, we prefer not to interfere. What would be the point of his lingering in pain? In that case, we'll ease his suffering as best we can and leave everything to nature."

"Does Irene think you can cure him?" Damon asked, suddenly worried. He realized what a terrible responsibility the Drakes had. The townspeople were used to their eccentricities and believed they were miracle workers.

"She wants to believe it. If Libby and my other sisters were here, all of us together might really be of some help, but the most we can do is slow things down to buy him time. We'll find out from Drew what he wants. You'll have to distract Irene for us. Have her go into the kitchen and make us lemonade and her famous cookies. She'll be anxious, Damon, so you'll really have to work at it. We'll need time with Drew."

His gaze narrowed as he studied Sarah's serious face. "What about you and your sisters? Are you going to be ill like you were last time?"

"Only if we work on him," Sarah said. "Then I don't know how you'll get us all home. You'll have to ask Irene to drive us back."

"We should have thought to bring the car," Kate agreed. "Do you think that's a bad omen? Maybe there's nothing we can do."

"Don't go thinking that way, Kate," Abbey reprimanded. "We all love to walk and it's fun to be together. We can do this. If we're lucky we can buy Drew enough time to allow Libby to come home."

"Is Libby coming back?" Damon asked.

"I don't know, Damon," Hannah said, her eyebrow raising, "that's rather up to you, now, isn't it?"

"Why would it be up to me?"

"I thought you said he was one of the smartest men on the planet," Kate teased. "Didn't you design some top-secret defense system?"

Damon glared at the women, at Sarah. "If I did and it was top secret, no one would know, now would they?"

Hannah laughed. "Don't be angry, Damon, Sarah didn't tell us. We share knowledge, sort of like a collective pool. I can't tell you how it works, only that we all have it. She would never give out that kind of information, even to us. It just happens. None of us would say anything, well," she hedged, "except to tease you."

"So why is it up to me whether or not Libby comes home?"

"She'll come home if there's a wedding," Kate pointed out with a grin.

Chapter 12

DAMON LOOKED AROUND him at the four pale faces. Each of the Drake sisters was lying on a couch or draped over a chair, exhaustion written into the lines of her face. For a moment he felt helpless in the midst of their weariness, not knowing what to do for them. They had sat in Irene's car, not speaking, with their white faces and trembling bodies. He had barely managed to help them into the cliff house.

The phone rang, the sound shrill in the complete stillness of the house. The women didn't move or turn toward the sound so Damon picked up the receiver. "Yes?"

There was a long pause. "You must be Damon." The voice was like a caress of velvet. "What's wrong with them? I can feel them all the way here." The voice didn't say where "here" was.

"You're a sister?"

"Of course." Impatience now. "Elle. What's wrong with them?"

"They went to Irene's to see Drew." Damon could hear the sheer relief in the small sigh on the other end.

"Make them sweet tea. There's a canister in the cupboard right above the stove, marked MAGIC." Damon carried the phone with him into the kitchen. "Drop a couple of teaspoons of the powder into the teapot and let the tea steep. That will help. Is the house warm? If not, get it warm: build a fire and use the furnace, whatever it takes. When's the wedding?"

"How soon can you and your sisters get back home?" Damon asked.

"You know I should be angry with you. Not that burner, use the back burner. That's the right canister."

"I don't see what difference a burner makes, but okay and why should you be upset with me?" He didn't even wonder how she knew what he was doing or what burner he was using. He took it as a matter of course.

"Because I'm concentrating on it, the burner I mean. As for being upset, I think you started something we have no control over. I have no intention of finding a man for a long while. I have things to do with my life and a man doesn't come into it, thank you very much. The infuser is in the very bottom drawer to the left of the sink." She spoke as if she could see him going through the drawers looking for the little infuser to put the tea in.

The house shuddered. Stilled. A ripple of alarm went through Damon.

"What was that?" Elle sounded anxious again.

"An earthquake maybe. A minor one. I've got the kettle on, the teapot is ready with the powder, two teaspoons of this stuff? Have you smelled it lately?" Damon was tempted to taste it. "It isn't a dragon's liver, is it?"

Elle laughed. "We save those for Harrington. When he drops by we put it in his coffee."

"I really feel sorry for that man." To his astonishment the teakettle shrilled loudly almost immediately. He poured the water into the little teapot and tossed a tea towel over it for added warmth. "Are you really going to have seven daughters?" he asked curiously, amazed that anyone would even consider it. Amazed that he was talking comfortably to a virtual stranger.

The house shuddered a second time. A branch scraped along an outside wall with an eerie sound. The wind moaned and rattled the windows.

"So the prophecy says," Elle replied with a small sigh of resignation. "Damon, is something else wrong there?"

"No, they're just very tired." Damon poured the tea into four cups and set the cups on a tray. "And the house keeps shaking."

"Hang up and call the sheriff's office," Elle said urgently. "Do it now."

He caught the sudden alarm in her voice and a chill went down his spine. Damn them all for their psychic nonsense. There wasn't really anything wrong, was there?

The dogs roared a vicious challenge. The animals were in the front yard, inside the fence, yet they were hurling their bodies against the front door so hard the wood threatened to splinter. Damon did as Elle commanded and phoned the sheriff's office for help.

No one screamed. Most women might have screamed under the circumstances but none of them did. When he carried the tray into the living room, all four of the Drake sisters were sitting quietly in their chairs. He ignored the two men standing in the middle of the room with guns drawn. Where before, when confronted with guns and violence, he had panicked, this time he remained quite calm.

He knew they were killers. He knew what to expect. And this time, he knew he wouldn't allow them to hurt the Drake sisters. It was very simple to him. It didn't matter to him if he died, he needed the women to survive and live in the world. They were the ones who mattered, all that mattered. The women *would* remain alive.

Damon set the tray on the coffee table and handed each of the sisters a cup of tea before turning to face the two men. He remembered them in vivid detail. The man with the swollen jaw had taken pleasure in torturing him. Damon was glad he had swung his cane hard enough to fracture the jaw.

Damon straightened slowly. These men had murdered for the knowledge Damon carried in his brain. They had crippled him permanently and changed his entire life. Now they stood in Sarah's home, sheer blasphemy on their part. They had entered through the sliding-glass door and had left it open behind them.

Outside, the sea appeared calm, but he could see, in the distance, small frothy waves gathering and rolling with a building boom on the open water. He felt power moving him, a connection with the women through Sarah. Beloved, mysterious Sarah. He waited while the women sipped their tea. Stalling for time, knowing exactly what he would do.

"You two seem to keep turning up," Damon finally greeted. He took two steps to his right, closer to Sarah, turning slightly sideways so she could see the small gun he had taken from the hidden drawer where Elle had said he would find it. "Do you not have homes and families to go to?"

"Shut up, Wilder. You know what we want. This time we have someone you care about. When I put a gun to her head I think you're going to tell me what I want to know."

Damon looked past the man to the rolling sea. The wind was gusting, chopping the surface into white foam. The waves crested higher. The dogs continued roaring with fury and shaking the foundations of the living room door. Damon calmly raked his fingers through his hair, his gaze on a distant point beyond the men. The sisters drank the hot sweet revitalizing tea. And the power moved through Damon stronger than ever. Around each man a strange shadow flitted back and forth. A black circle that seemed to surround first one, then the other. At times the shadow appeared to have a human form. Most of the time it was insubstantial.

"Would you care for a cup of tea?" Sarah asked politely. "We have plenty."

"Do sit down," Kate invited. She shifted position, a subtle movement hardly noticeable, but it put her body slightly between the guns and Hannah.

"This gun is real," the man with the swollen jaw snapped. "This isn't a party." He grinned evilly at his partner. "Although when it's over we might take one or two of the women with us for the road."

Sarah looked bored. "It's very obvious neither of you is the brains in this venture. I can't imagine that the man in jail is, either. Who in the world would hire such comedians to go looking for national secrets? It's almost ludicrous. Are you in trouble with your boss and he's looking to get rid of you?"

"You have a smart mouth, lady; it won't be so hard to shoot you."

"Do have some tea, at least we can be civil," Abbey said sweetly. There was a strange cadence to her voice, a singsong quality that pulled at the listeners, drew them into her suggestions. "If you're going to be with us for some time, we may as well enjoy ourselves with a fine cup of tea first and get to know one another."

The air in the room was fresh, almost perfumed, yet smelled of the sea, crisp and clean and salty. The two men looked confused, blinking rapidly, and exchanged a long bewildered frown. The man with the swollen jaw actually lowered his gun and took a step toward the tray with the little teapot.

Kate stared intently at the locks on the front door, and the knob itself. Sarah never took her eyes from the two men. Waiting. Watching. The huntress. Damon thought of her that way. Listening, he thought he heard music, far out over the sea. Music in the wind. A soft melodious song calling to the elements. All the while the dark shadow edged around the two intruders.

Hannah lifted her arms to the back of the couch, a graceful, elegant motion. The wind rose to a shriek, burst into the room with the force of a freight train. The men staggered under the assault, the wind ripping at their clothing. The bolt on the door turned and the door burst open under the heavy weight of the dogs. The animals leapt inside, teeth bared. Damon blinked as the crouching shadow leapt onto the back of one of the men and remained there.

Sarah was already in motion, diving at the two men, going in low to catch the first man in a scissor kick, rolling to bring him down. He toppled into his partner, knocking him down so that his head slammed against the base of a chair. Sarah caught the gun Damon threw to her.

The man with the swollen jaw rose up, throwing the chair as he drew a second gun. Damon attempted a kick with his one good leg. Sarah fired off three rounds, the bullets driving the man backward and away from Damon. She calmly pressed the hot barrel against the temple of the intruder on the floor. "I suggest you don't move." But she was looking at the man she shot, watching Hannah and Abbey trying to revive him. Watching the dark shadow steal away, dragging with it something heavy. Knowing her sisters could not undo what she had done. Sarah wiped her forehead with her palm and blinked back tears.

Kate collected the guns. Abbey held back the dogs by simply placing her hand in warning on their heads.

"I'm sorry, Sarah," Damon said.

"It was necessary." She felt sick. It didn't matter that he'd intended to kill them all, or that Death had been satisfied. She had taken a life.

The wind moved through the room again, a soft breeze this time, bringing music with it. Touching Sarah. She looked at her sisters and smiled tiredly. "Hannah, the cavalry is coming up the drive. Do let them in and don't do anything you'll regret later."

Hannah rolled her eyes, stomped across the room, landing a frustrated kick to the shins on the man Sarah was holding. "Thanks a lot, I have to see that giant skunk two times in one day. That's more than any lady should have to deal with."

Abigail leaned down, her face level with Sarah's prisoner. "You'd really like to tell me who you're working for, wouldn't you?" Her tone was sweet, hypnotic, compelling. She looked directly into his eyes, holding him captive there. Waiting for the name. Waiting for the truth.

At the doorway, Hannah called out a greeting to Jonas Harrington. "As usual, you're just a bit on the late side. Still haven't quite gotten over that bad habit of being late you set in school. You always did like to make your entrance at least ten minutes after the bell." She had her hand on her hip and she tossed the silky mass of wavy hair tumbling around her shoulders. "It was juvenile then and it's criminal now."

Deliberately he stepped in close to her, crowding her with his much larger body. "Someone should have turned you over their knee a long time ago." The words were too low for anyone else to hear and he was sweeping past her to enter the room. Just for a moment his glittering eyes slashed at her, burned her.

Every woman in the room reacted, eyes glaring at Jonas. Hannah held up her hand in silent admission she'd provoked him. She allowed the rest of the officers into the room before she took the dogs into the bedroom. Damon noticed she didn't return.

All the women were exhausted. Damon wanted everyone else gone. It seemed more important to push more tea into the Drake sisters' hands, to tuck blankets around them, to shield them from prying eyes when they were obviously so vulnerable. He stayed close to Sarah while she was questioned repeatedly. The medical examiner removed the body and the crime scene team went over the room.

Each of the sisters gave a separate report so it seemed an eternity until Damon had the house back in his control. "Thanks, Abbey, I don't know how you managed to get that name, but hopefully they'll be able to stop anyone else from coming after me."

Abbey closed her eyes and laid her head against the back-rest of the chair. "It was my pleasure. Will you answer the phone? Tell Elle we're too tired to talk but have her tell the others we're all right."

"The phone isn't ringing." But he was already walking into the kitchen to answer it. Of course it wasn't ringing. Yet. But it would. And it did. And he reassured Elle he wouldn't leave her sisters and all was well in their world.

It seemed hours before he was alone with Sarah. His Sarah. Before he could frame her face in his hands and lower his head to kiss her with every bit of tenderness he had in him. "There was something I saw, a shadow, dark and grim. I felt it had been on me, with me, and now it's gone. That sounds ridiculous, Sarah, but I feel lighter, as if a great burden is off of me. You know what I'm talking about, don't you?"

"Yes." She said it simply.

His gaze moved possessively over her face. "You look so tired. I'd carry you to bed, but we wouldn't make it if I tried."

She managed a small smile. "It would be okay if you dropped me on the floor. I'd just go to sleep."

He helped her through the hall to the stairs. "Hannah has the turret leading to the battlement, doesn't she?"

Sarah was pleased that he knew. "The sea draws her. The wind and rain. It helps her to be there, up high, where she can see it all. I'm glad you understand."

He went up the stairs behind her, ready to break her fall should there be need. Ready to do whatever it took to protect her. "It surprises me that I feel the power in this house, but I do. I'm a scientist. None of this makes sense, what you and your sisters are. Hell, I don't even know how I'd describe you, but I know it's real."

"Stay with me tonight, Damon," Sarah said. "I feel very weary, like I'm stretched thin. When you're with me, I'm not so lost."

"You'd have to throw me out, Sarah," he replied truthfully. "I know I love you and I want you for my wife. I don't ever want us to be apart."

"I feel the same, Damon." Sarah pushed open the door to her bedroom and collapsed on the large four-poster bed. She looked beautiful to him, lying there, waiting for him to stretch out beside her.

Her window faced the sea. Damon could see the water, a deep blue, waves swelling high, collapsing, rushing the shores and receding as it had for so many years. Peace was in his heart and mind. Soft laughter came from various parts of the house. It swept through the air, and filled the house with joy. Sarah was back. Sarah was home. And Damon had come home with her.

New York Times **bestselling author**

Christine Feehan

OCEANS OF FIRE

A Drake Sisters Novel

The third daughter of seven in a magical bloodline, Abigail Drake was born with an affinity for water and a strong bond with dolphins. After she witnesses a murder, she flees right into the arms of Alexsandr Volstov.

On the trail of stolen Russian antiques, he's a relentless Interpol agent—and the man who had once broken Abby's heart. But he isn't going to let the only woman he's ever loved slip away again.

0-515-13953-X

Available wherever books are sold or at
penguin.com

New York Times bestselling author

CHRISTINE FEEHAN

MIND GAME

Dahlia LaBlanc's gifts are also a curse, making it impossible for her to be around others without hurting them. But can she trust her secrets to Nicholas Trevane, a Ghostwalker sent to find her?

0-515-13809-6

Praise for the novels of Christine Feehan:

"A skillful blend of supernatural thrills and romance that is sure to entice readers."
—*Publishers Weekly*

"Intense, sensual, and mesmerizing."
—*Library Journal*

And coming November 2005
NIGHT GAME

Available wherever books are sold or at penguin.com